BODY MAGIC

THE TRIAD OF MAGIC, BOOK TWO

MACY BLAKE
POPPY DENNISON

Body Magic

Cover Design by AJ Corza

AUTHOR'S NOTE

Body Magic was originally published in 2012 under a different name. I have revised and edited that edition and decided to consolidate to a single pen name, so am releasing it as Macy. I hope you all enjoy exploring the Triad of Magic as much as I enjoyed going back and experiencing it again. This series was the first thing I'd ever written, and I never imagined being a published author. It's hard to believe so much has changed in just a few short years.

The rhythmic thud of Rocky's fist hitting his boxing bag filtered out all other sound in the guest cabin he currently called home. Pain flared up his knuckles, through his arm, and into his shoulder with each strike. The punishing workout soothed his need to lash out in anger. He needed to hit something or someone, and the bag would suffice.

His cell phone rang, the trill ringtone a bitter reminder of his task. He considered ignoring it, but the consequences outweighed the annoyance. "Harris."

"What do you have to report?" His alpha, William Malone, had set Rocky on this task. He couldn't do less than fulfill his duty.

"Alpha Gray mated the mage."

Malone laughed. "Perfect. The Were Council will hear of this, I'm sure."

"Gray plans to report the news himself. They also killed a mage in an attack tonight."

"Even better. The High Moon Pack will have both the Conclave of Mages and the Were Council on their heads. The alpha doesn't stand a chance."

Which was exactly what Malone had hoped. Rocky's role as a

security specialist came with a double-edged sword. Yes, he upgraded security systems for packs all over the country. But at the same time, he learned their inner workings, their weaknesses, and reported the information to his alpha through the computer systems he installed. "Alpha Gray is vulnerable." Rocky's gut clenched again with the admission.

"I think we may have found the one to take over. What are your thoughts?"

Rocky fought back a disdain-filled snort. Malone couldn't care less about Rocky's thoughts. He'd do what he wanted regardless of Rocky's response. "You're right. They're weakened. The kidnapping of their cubs has shaken them to the core. Now with a mage serving as alpha-mate? Their faith in their alpha is waning."

"Perfect. What was your role in the attack? Did you witness the fight itself?"

"Yes, Alpha. I arranged with their pack alpha to serve as witness, but I did nothing to assist them, as you commanded." And Rocky had seen things he'd never imagined possible from his hiding spot. The mage had thrown the wolves around like toys. If the vampire hadn't killed him, they wouldn't have won the fight.

Pack tradition demanded the separation of magical species. Rocky understood why after what he'd witnessed.

"Tomorrow, I want you to offer reparation to the alpha for your cowardice. He'll be forced to contact me, and it will give me the in I'm looking for. Good work."

The praise settled cold and dark in Rocky's stomach. His role as a spy had never affected him so deeply, but he'd never come across a pack that could actually fall to his alpha's machinations.

"Thank you, Alpha."

The beep of the call ending was the only response he received. Rocky tossed his phone onto the couch and returned to his workout. He switched to his legs, hammering his knee repeatedly into the canvas until his thigh began to burn with strain. He may look skinny and weak, but he trained hard to make his body strong. It was the only way he could survive the life his alpha ordered him to live.

Gray's foolishness would be his downfall. It was bitter consolation, but all Rocky had. The alpha of this pack thought he was above the rules. Rocky scoffed. No one could throw away years of tradition without consequences. *Pack first.* The mantra all wolves lived by, and the one this pack's alpha had tossed so carelessly aside.

Rocky switched legs when his knee began to throb from the repeated hits. He'd just begun the repetitions on his right leg when the back of his neck began to tingle. Someone was close, watching.

What if they'd overheard his phone call? What if they were gathering the pack together now to deal with his betrayal?

"If you're going to stand there and stare, you might as well come in." Better to face them head-on than wait for the inevitable.

Rocky held the bag steady and continued using his knee to strike it. He glanced over his shoulder when the cabin door opened.

Cade let himself inside. "Didn't mean to spy. Heard some strange noises and thought I should check it out."

"Whatever, man." His thighs burning, Rocky stopped the set and raised his faded blue T-shirt to wipe the sweat from his face.

"So what was that you were doing?"

Rocky glared over the edge of his shirt. "Working. Out."

Something about the alpha's best friend rubbed him the wrong way. Another loyal puppy, following whatever Gray said, no matter the consequences. Some best friend. Cade should be leading the force to get Gray to come to his senses.

Instead, he stood in Rocky's cabin, his muscled arms crossed over his broad chest. Not many men intimidated Rocky with their sheer size, but Cade did. Next to Cade, Rocky looked pale and lanky. Ordinary.

"What the hell is your issue? You've had nothing but attitude with me since you got here."

Rocky gave the bag another brutal punch and turned to face Cade. He stalked over to him and stopped inches away from Cade's face. "My issue is you and this pack. I'm simply giddy over the fact that we almost died tonight at the hands of a rogue mage, and yet your alpha, in all of his infinite wisdom, chose to mate one anyway."

Cade growled deep in his chest. "Then why don't you leave? I'll be happy to help." He took the last step forward so he and Rocky stood nose to nose.

Rocky would love to get the hell out of Tennessee and head back West where packs made sense and demons and mages stayed away from them, as the law commanded. He couldn't do that without going against his alpha's demands. Rocky had learned a long time ago not to cross Malone.

Rocky pushed even closer. "I'd like to see you try."

At six four and two hundred forty pounds, Cade was the largest member of the High Moon Pack, even bigger than his alpha, and the quintessential tough guy. After the night Rocky had just experienced, he wasn't in the mood to deal with any of Cade's macho bullshit.

Cade didn't seem to be in the mood either. He grabbed Rocky in his massive arms and squeezed. Rocky let out a choked gasp. Fuck, Cade was just as strong as he looked.

Rocky leaned sharply to the side and raised his knee in a quick jab that nailed Cade right in the nuts. Cade choked out a gasp of pain and loosened his hold. It was enough for Rocky to twist free. He punched Cade in the throat and jammed his knee up into Cade's ribcage.

With a pain-filled grunt, Cade hunched over. Rocky swung his arm around, and it cracked against Cade's jaw. Cade rolled backward with the hit and spun around as he shifted to his wolf form. He leapt in a fluid motion, one moment a man, the next a wolf. Rocky had never seen anyone shift that fast. His moment of hesitation cost him, and Cade took him down.

Cade held Rocky by the throat with his mouth, his teeth sharp against the tender skin of Rocky's human neck. One snap of Cade's powerful jaws and Rocky's days of spying would be over.

Rocky forced out a breath and shifted. His transformation took longer, as to be expected from a wolf of his status. The lowest of the low. No way could he shift in midleap like Cade had.

Cade held on, his breath warm even through the fur now covering Rocky's throat. As a man, the size difference between them wasn't much, but Cade's wolf dwarfed Rocky's. Another sign of his weakness.

Cade shook his head enough to make sure he had Rocky's full attention without doing any real damage. Rocky shuddered and arched his neck in submission. With one final tug to reinforce his point, Cade released his hold on Rocky. He shifted again, returning to his human form as quickly as he'd managed the transformation to his wolf.

After a few tense moments, Rocky shifted as well. He lay naked and breathless on the floor. A trickle of something wet slid down his throat, and Rocky swiped at it. His fingers came away red with his own blood.

Cade's teeth had broken through the skin of his neck and left a small bite mark on his nape. Cade stood back, watching to see what Rocky's reaction to being taken down would be.

Rocky stayed put, not needing another example of Cade's strength and speed. He could blame his takedown on the difference in their wolves, claim that all the reds were smaller, like him. The High Moon Pack consisted of gray wolves, and most of them easily weighed two hundred pounds when they shifted. Rocky's smaller wolf weighed much less, maybe one fifty if he was lucky. The rusty reddish-brown of his wolf's coat matched his human hair.

In reality, the breed of wolf made no difference. Rocky's human stature had nothing to do with his wolf form. He'd worked for years to make the most of his slender frame, adding bulk where he could and honing his fighting skills.

Still, his wolf had few defenses against a wolf of Cade's ability, no matter the size. Rocky rolled to his feet and impatiently flicked at the wound on his neck. He returned to the hanging bag and punched it viciously. The bolts holding it to the ceiling gave an ominous creak. Rocky leaned his head against the black leather and let out a frustrated growl.

Cade gave him a moment to pull himself together. "Okay, let's just, I don't know... Stop, I guess." He walked over to the opposite side of the bag and wrapped his hands around the sides. "Show me how to do that knee thing you were doing."

Rocky looked up, and their eyes met. "What?" he sputtered.

"You know, that cool knee thing. How'd you do that so fast? I don't think I could keep my balance."

Rocky shook his head in confusion, and his shaggy hair dropped into his face. Why wasn't Cade lording his win over Rocky? Making it clear who'd won that battle for dominance?

He adjusted his stance and kneed the bag. "That?" He didn't raise his eyes when he asked. He didn't need to antagonize Cade.

"Yeah. But you did like, fifty of them in a row before. I want to learn how to do that."

"Okay." Rocky paused and gathered his thoughts. He might not understand Cade's attitude, but working out, he got. "Well, it's in your stance. You have to keep your base leg at an angle and keep your feet a bit more than shoulder width apart. Uh, just give it a try, and I'll show you."

Cade nodded and used his leg to hit the bag. After the third rep, he lost his balance and had to step back. "See?"

"Yeah. You aren't setting up correctly. Here, let me show you." Rocky came around behind Cade and reached out for his waist. Skin met skin. They were both still naked after their shift. "Uh, let me put my shorts on first."

Cade shrugged. "Sure."

"I'll grab you some too." Cade's jeans lay in a tangled heap by the door where he'd shifted. Skintight denim didn't suit a workout of knee jabs.

"Okay."

Nudity didn't bother most shifters. Part of being a shifter meant you got naked in front of other people. At least their clothes didn't rip to shreds like in the horror movies. Must be the magic. They just sort of fell away.

Rocky had always been self-conscious of his smaller size, and didn't care to wander around naked, even though he wasn't the same scrawny boy he had been. The barrier of clothes made him feel safer. He ignored his discarded clothes on the floor and left Cade in the living room. Once in his bedroom, he took a deep, calming breath before he slipped on a pair of loose gray sweatpants and grabbed a pair of green shorts for Cade.

He went back to the other room and tossed the shorts to Cade. "Those should work. They're a bit big on me."

Cade stepped into the shorts and pulled them up. They were snug and didn't leave much to the imagination, but Rocky was more comfortable with them both covered.

"Thanks." Cade's stance relaxed, and he stared at Rocky for a long moment. "Look, it's no secret I'm not happy we had to bring in an outsider for security."

"I know," Rocky said and turned to the bag. "You've made it very clear."

"But I will admit we're in over our heads with all this and could use the upgrades."

An understatement if Rocky had ever heard one. When you lay down with dogs, you ended up with fleas. Being this close to a mage had Rocky itching already. He had to play along with Cade to keep the peace and get his job done, though. "Agreed."

"So, how about we call a truce. I'll try to keep my attitude in check if you'll do the same."

"Yeah." Rocky wouldn't make any promises, but he'd try to keep his mouth shut. Which meant changing the subject. "Okay—now your stance. Get set up again."

Cade complied. Rocky stepped up behind him and put his hands on Cade's hips. "Here, twist your hips a bit to the side." When Cade moved too far, Rocky stopped him with a gentle squeeze. "No, not that much. There. Now slide your foot a little more so it's angled away from you."

"Like this?"

Rocky nodded. "Good. Now, try."

Cade kicked the bag again, repeating the motion several times before he began to lose his balance. He dropped his foot back to the ground. "I still couldn't do as many as you."

Rocky chuckled a bit. "Well, I've been doing knee jabs for years.

Besides, you aren't holding your stomach tight enough." Rocky stepped a little to the side and put his hand on Cade's waist. "Here, do it again. But this time, focus on keeping these muscles tight. Right where my hand is."

They both looked down at Rocky's hand on Cade's stomach. Cade's muscles flexed, the deep brown of his skin a sharp contrast against Rocky's pale fingers. The borrowed green shorts developed a distinct bulge in the front. Cade tried to turn his body to hide his reaction, clearly embarrassed over his body's response to Rocky.

Rocky pretended not to see, but his sweats couldn't hide his own body's response to Cade's attraction. Damn hormones. Rocky blamed Gray and the whole mating thing happening just up the hill. Even if the mage was an inappropriate mate, the allure of a newly mated pair sent hormones raging throughout a pack. *Right.* Rocky would stick to that theory.

"No, don't turn like that," Rocky said and tightened his hold. Cade stumbled and grabbed the bag to keep himself from falling over. "Keep your hips straight."

Damn. The thick scent of arousal filled the air. Rocky's sweats tented more in response. He brushed up against Cade, his cock brushing against Cade's ass. "Yeah, like that," Rocky mumbled.

He forced his horny brain to stop his train of thought in its tracks. Cade gave the bag a couple halfhearted kicks, but if his dick was half as hard as Rocky's, he wasn't very comfortable right now.

"Okay, man. That was helpful. You think you can show me a few more tricks sometime?" Cade kept his back to Rocky, but awareness sizzled between them.

"Yeah, sure." If his hormones kept this up, he'd love to show Cade a few of his tricks.

"Well, I'm going to head back to my place. It's pretty late. See you tomorrow." Cade let go of the bag and went for the door. He stooped to pick up his discarded clothes along the way. "Care if I just bring these shorts back tomorrow?"

"No problem." Rocky hesitated, then decided to take a risk. "Hey, Cade?"

Cade paused with his hand on the doorknob. "Yeah?"

"If I show you how to do some of this martial arts stuff, do you think you could teach me how to shift as fast as you did earlier?"

Cade looked back over his shoulder, careful to keep his hips out of Rocky's line of sight.

Rocky couldn't quite figure out what the look in Cade's eyes meant, but something had changed between them. Maybe Rocky's submission or their bodies' reactions to each other. "Sure. I'll help you."

Rocky looked down and blew out a long breath. "Thanks."

"Night, Rocky. Get some sleep."

Rocky waited until Cade walked out of sight of his cabin and went straight for the shower. He left his sweats in a crumpled heap on the white tile floor and turned the water on as hot as he could stand it. He tried to ignore the sensations the water gave him as it pounded down on his dick, but it didn't work. After a few minutes of heightened awareness, he grabbed the conditioner and poured a glob in his hand.

It didn't take long, only a few hard strokes, before he spurted his release over the shower wall. He didn't acknowledge that memories of his hands on Cade's hips—or that mysterious look in Cade's eyes—had anything to do with his orgasm.

2

*S*imon woke up with a grimace. Stupid thirty in the morning and his body insisted he get moving, as usual. His body clock didn't seem to care that Thomas, the mage who was training him, had almost killed Simon the day before, or that he'd spent half the night getting to know his new werewolf mate in an up close and personal kind of way.

The intensity of sex with Gray blew Simon's mind. He hadn't known it could be more than a simple physical connection. *Simple.* Simon grinned as his entire body reminded him that there was nothing simple about his mating. He yawned and stretched. With the kind of workout Gray had given him the night before, the least his body could do was let him get a little rest to recuperate. He cracked open one eye and checked the clock on the nightstand. Six forty-five. Whoa. He'd slept in for fifteen whole minutes.

Simon wasn't quite ready to climb out of bed. He glanced over to his left and watched his new mate sleeping. Gray had stolen the dark blue comforter during the night and had it wrapped around him like a cocoon. Only the top of his head poked out from beneath the covers. The short gray hair of his military-style crew cut tempted Simon's fingers. He'd already developed a fondness for tickling the soft strands against his palm.

Gray had taken over most of the bed during the night. Sleeping with someone else would definitely take some adjustment. As it was, Simon had just enough room at the edge of the mattress. Any farther, and he'd be on the floor. Gray huffed out a snuffling half snore and rolled over. More of his face was visible now. Simon took the opportunity to observe Gray without his mate's knowing gaze staring back at him.

In sleep, Gray appeared less intense. With his startling blue eyes covered, Gray certainly didn't resemble an intimidating alpha werewolf. Even the little line that appeared on his forehead when he worried smoothed out while he rested. But Gray didn't really scare Simon. Well, he had the first day they'd met, when Simon had returned Gray's kidnapped son. Oh, the look he'd gotten that day had about given Simon a heart attack. Well, maybe just a panic attack. Close enough.

But when it came down to it, and Simon had been bleeding on the ground from the wounds Thomas had inflicted on him, he'd had to make a choice. Either let Cormac, the vampire he'd just learned was a distant relative, turn him into a vampire or accept Gray's offer of becoming his mate.

The choice hadn't been too difficult. Something about the werewolf drew Simon in. He had no idea what kind of trouble they'd gotten themselves into by breaking the laws of both the mages and the weres like this. Not to mention that Simon had no idea how to be a good partner, much less an alpha-mate.

Simon heard the sound of the toilet flushing in the hall bathroom, then water running. A few seconds later, quiet footsteps came toward the bedroom door. When no one knocked, Simon slipped out of bed and went over to the door. He opened it a crack and saw Garon standing outside looking hesitant to disturb them.

"Morning, buddy. You okay?"

"Yeah. Just wondered if you and Dad wanted to come have breakfast with me."

"Sure. Your dad's still asleep, but I'll come with you. Let me put a shirt on. I'll be right back."

Garon smiled and nodded. The little boy had been through so much lately. The kidnapping had affected Garon more than some of the other children. The demon who had taken them had left a draining spell in the boy that almost killed him. Simon had been able to remove the spell in time, but it had been very close.

That he'd be happy to spend time with Simon, and not just his dad, filled Simon with a kind of pride he'd never felt before. Simon returned Garon's smile, then turned back to the bedroom. He left the door open to let in a sliver of light and looked around the bedroom floor for his shirt. He couldn't find it, but he did locate Gray's. He scooped it up and slipped the soft fabric over his head. It was too big, one of Gray's standard plain ones that he wore like a uniform. It was comfortable enough to wear downstairs, and that's all Simon cared about.

When he went back out the door, Garon stared at the shirt for a second before laughing and looking up at Simon. "You look funny."

"No, I don't. You look funny."

Garon laughed again and tugged on the hem of the T-shirt. "You're wearing Dad's shirt."

"Yeah, well... I couldn't find mine."

"Aunt Maggie says if you put your clothes away like you're supposed to, you wouldn't have to search everywhere for what you wanted."

Simon tried not to laugh. He was pretty sure Maggie wouldn't appreciate finding their clothes scattered all over creation after the frantic way he and Gray had tossed them around the night before. He'd have to remember to straighten up later. "She sure is a smart lady."

They made it down to the kitchen. Garon slumped down at the counter with a huge sigh. "I don't want cereal."

"Okay. What do you want?"

His little head popped up and a lock of his dark brown hair fell over his forehead. "You mean I don't have to have cereal?"

"Not if you don't want it. Why?"

"'Cause Dad only cooks on the grill. And he doesn't exactly like mornings."

Simon chuckled. "Well, let's see what we can find. What are you in the mood for?"

"Waffles. With blueberry syrup. And whipped cream."

"Okay." Simon looked around the kitchen, wondering where to start searching for a waffle iron. Garon came around the counter and opened up the cabinet by the stove. He pulled out the appliance with a grin and handed it over. "Thanks. Now what else?"

"We need the mix stuff." Garon pushed his hair aside and looked up at Simon expectantly.

"Right. And where would that be?"

Garon ran over to the pantry and grabbed a box from the shelf while Simon got the waffle iron plugged in and heated up. When he handed the mix over, Simon grinned. "Now a bowl."

They shared a silly grin, and Garon pointed to an upper cabinet. Simon opened it up and pulled a large bowl from the top shelf.

"We need that spray stuff too. Aunt Maggie says they'll stick and make a mess if you don't use it."

"Well, let's get the spray, then!"

"I'm on it!"

Simon read the directions on the mix and then dumped some in the bowl. He added water and stirred it up, thankful that this was one of the easy-to-make varieties.

Garon pulled the lid off the spray, and Simon opened the now hot waffle iron. He nodded for Garon to go ahead, and Garon doused the black plates with the nonstick spray. Simon poured some of the mix into the center of the checkered design and closed the top.

"Hey, Simon. Can I ask you something?"

"Sure." Simon checked the time on the microwave and read the instructions for how long the waffle needed to cook.

"Um, are you and my dad, you know, like having sex and stuff?"

Blood heated Simon's skin and crept up his neck. His heart pounded, and he shifted uncomfortably.

"Well, your dad and I are mates now." He set the box of waffle mix back on the counter and tried to muster up a smile. Unsure if he should be having this conversation, Simon sent out a call for help. *Gray! Wake up!* Having a mind-link with your mate at a time like this? Priceless.

Wha? Huh? I'm up! What's wrong?

Nothing, but I need you in the kitchen, please.

Simon heard the thump of feet hitting the floor upstairs and checked on the waffle. "Another minute or so," he said to Garon.

"Yeah. I didn't mean to make you mad."

Simon turned to him and realized just how upset Garon looked. "Hey, Gar. I'm not mad, okay? I promise. I guess I just wasn't sure what to say. It's kind of grown-up stuff, you know?"

"Yeah. I just want my dad to be happy. One of the big kids says that Dad needs sex 'cause he's the alpha."

Fortunately, Gray entered the kitchen in time to hear Garon's statement. "Morning, kiddo. You talking about me?" Gray ruffled Garon's hair, then pulled him into a quick hug. Garon wrapped his arms around Gray's waist and leaned against him.

"Will you be mad at me?"

"For what? Asking questions? You know better than that. You can ask me whatever you want. If I can answer, I will. Deal?"

Simon turned back to the waffle. Golden brown. He pulled it off the maker and placed it on a plate. The next bit of mix sizzled on the hot metal as he poured it on and closed the lid again. He looked back to see Garon with his face buried against Gray's stomach.

"You're mated now, right, Dad?"

"Yep. Simon and I are mated." Simon noted Gray's slight smile when he said the words. Their eyes met for a moment, and Simon couldn't help but grin in return.

"Does that mean you have sex?"

Gray froze for a moment but then tightened his hold on his son and rubbed a hand down his back. "That's part of what being mated is, yes. But it's a lot more than that too."

Garon looked over at Simon, as if he were checking to make sure

Simon was okay with the discussion. Simon smiled at him and gave a little nod to let him know everything was fine.

"Robbie said you have to have sex 'cause you're the alpha."

"Well…" Gray paused to consider his words. "I'd like to think that being the alpha doesn't have anything to do with it, to be honest with you, son. Sex is something most grown-ups need, not just alphas."

"So all grown-ups have sex?" Garon tilted his head to the side in confusion.

"Pretty much."

"Even Grandpa and Mimi?"

"Even them."

"Whoa."

Simon smothered a laugh and pulled the next waffle out of the waffle iron. Gray wouldn't want one this early. When Simon had stayed with them while Gray and the pack searched for the demon who had kidnapped Garon, he had learned that Gray didn't eat until after he had his daily dose of caffeine. Simon grabbed the carafe from the coffeemaker and filled it with water. After adding it to the brewer, he dropped in a filter and added the strongest grounds he could find. He figured his mate would need a big pot of liquid energy after this talk.

When the coffee began dripping, Simon removed a couple plates from the cabinet and set them on the counter with a couple forks. Garon and Gray both watched him moving around the kitchen. Simon couldn't read anything negative in their expressions, but all of a sudden, he felt like he shouldn't be there. Maybe he'd crossed some strange line by making himself at home? Being in and out of the compound over the past couple weeks, he knew his way around. But actually stepping up and diving right in? Maybe he shouldn't. Simon needed to think about his role here. Although he really needed to finish making breakfast first.

Set on this plan, Simon crossed the kitchen to the freezer and stuck the bag of coffee inside where he'd found it. He wanted to get out the milk and juice for himself and Garon.

"Dad? Being a mate is a big deal, right?"

Simon froze in place, the refrigerator door open in his hand.

"It is a big deal. A very big deal."

"Yeah, I figured. So Simon gets to stay with us forever now, right?"

"That's the plan."

Forever? It shocked Simon in a way. He hadn't really considered the ramifications of agreeing to become Gray's mate. They barely knew each other. It had seemed like a good idea at the time, when he was broken and bleeding and had to make a choice. But with that simple statement, reality began to set in. Was he Garon's… stepfather? His grip on the door handle tightened, and Simon leaned into the cool air from the fridge to help cool his suddenly overheated face.

"I like you, Simon. I'm glad you're going to stay with us."

Simon located the blueberry syrup on one of the shelves in the door and grabbed it. He closed the door and noticed his blurred reflection in the stainless-steel panel. "Me too," he said, but he wasn't entirely sure he meant it.

Sure, the sex was fantastic, and he loved the feeling of family he got from the pack. But he'd known them less than a month. How could he make a forever commitment when he barely knew Gray? When he didn't even know what being the mate of an alpha entailed?

His heart began to pound, and his hands shook as he carried the syrup over to the counter.

"You forgot the whipped cream!" Garon let go of his dad and ran over to get the can himself.

"Sorry, buddy."

"That's okay." Garon sent a sly look his dad's way. "Can I put a lot on?"

Gray laughed and shook his head. "Not a lot. Maybe medium. Save some for Simon."

Garon stabbed a waffle and put it on his plate, then drowned it in syrup with a gleeful grin. He shook up the whipped cream and squirted the frothy white confection all over the top.

Simon leaned against the counter in an attempt to calm his quaking nerves.

You okay? Gray's voice in his mind sounded loud in the otherwise quiet room.

Oh, yeah. I'm fine.

Simon?

Right. A bold-faced lie on day one of their mating probably wasn't the best way to start their relationship. *Um, not okay. A little freaked out. Give me a minute?*

Sure. I'm right here if you need me.

Simon needed to know if he'd done the right thing. Needed to see that the reality of their choice wasn't going to come crashing down around them. Needed to understand what he'd gotten himself into.

He looked over at Gray. His mate leaned against the counter, wearing ratty sweatpants and a tight T-shirt. He sipped his coffee with his eyes closed, sheer pleasure from the hot brew clear on his face. Simon closed the fridge and walked over into Gray's arms. Gray moved the mug out of the way before it could spill and pulled Simon close. Maybe all he really needed was right here in front of him.

3

A brisk spring wind blew over Cade's bald head as he walked over to his alpha's house. He shivered and pulled a camouflage bandanna out of the back pocket of his faded jeans. As much as he liked the ease of keeping his head shaved, the instant chill made him wish for a little hair to keep his scalp warm.

Gray had called Cade and Liam up to the house this morning to debrief from the night before. Cade stopped by Liam's cabin and whistled to let the pack beta know he was there. Liam stepped out of the house, his dark hair still damp from a shower.

"You look tired."

Cade shrugged. "Long night."

Liam slapped a hand on Cade's shoulder and gave it a squeeze. "I couldn't sleep. Ended up patrolling for a couple hours."

"Me too."

The easy familiarity of their friendship helped Cade relax. The three of them had grown up together in the pack. Although Gray and Liam were a year older than Cade, they'd all been inseparable throughout their childhood. Since Gray was the alpha-heir at the time, Liam and Cade had trained with him. When Gray took over the leadership of the pack, his best friends remained at his side.

Liam snickered. "Did you happen to walk past Gray's last night?"

"Yeah. It was quiet everywhere else. Who knew Simon was a screamer?"

They both laughed and continued their walk up to Gray's house. "Should we give him hell about it?"

"Definitely."

As they approached the cabin where the cubs attended school, a shiver of guilt raced up Cade's spine. If only he'd been there like he was supposed to be. Maybe he'd have been able to stop the demon before it took the cubs.

Liam bumped his shoulder against Cade's. "Stop. It wasn't your fault."

Cade tore his gaze away from the school and looked back at Liam. "Am I the only one freaking out about all this?"

"God, no. Look, I know you're as happy for Gray as I am. But mating a mage? It raises a lot of concerns we'll have to address as a pack. The Were Council will get involved, and we'll need to be ready to defend Gray's choice to break pack law."

The ripple effect from Gray and Simon's mating would probably cause a tsunami's worth of shit to come back on them. They'd tossed aside law, tradition, everything.

Cade didn't really understand why the restrictions were there in the first place. "Do you think Simon will know more from the mage side of things? Seems like there has to be a reason it's forbidden. Somebody has to know."

Gray's house appeared from behind the trees at the end of the path. "Let's hope so."

Cade wondered if he should have taken his life in a different direction. School and Cade hadn't gotten along very well, so he'd gone on to a short trade program after he'd graduated from high school. He worked as a handyman in town and handled all the routine maintenance around the pack's compound.

His business gave him the flexibility to do more work for the pack. He took on extra patrol shifts. Maybe he should have fought his way through school and gotten a degree from a fancy university like Liam and Gray had. Might be nice to be useful when they needed something other than his size and speed. Whenever Gray needed pure force at his side, he always chose Cade. Though at times like this, it didn't seem to be enough.

Liam knocked on Gray's door, and the alpha answered a few moments later.

"Morning, guys. Come on in."

They followed Gray into the kitchen where Garon and Simon sat chatting. Gray refilled his coffee mug and poured Liam and Cade cups as well. Simon glanced over at them and gave them a quick smile.

"I'm going to go meditate. Back in a few."

Gray tugged Simon close before he could get away and nuzzled his hair. Simon pulled away after a moment and hurried from the room. Cade could smell the arousal in the air and chuckled.

"What's funny?" Garon asked.

Gray started laughing and shook his head.

"Sorry, buddy," Cade answered. "I was just laughing at your dad being *up* this early."

Liam turned away, and Cade could see his shoulders shaking.

"You guys are weird. Dad, can I go get dressed?"

"Go ahead. And brush your teeth."

Garon went upstairs, and the three friends remained in the kitchen. Gray glared at Cade before breaking into a smile.

"So… have fun last night?" Cade burst out laughing, unable to keep it inside.

"Shut it." Gray started to refill his coffee again, but it was still full.

Liam smirked. "Uh-huh. *Someone* had lots of fun. And we know this because *someone* was really loud about it."

Gray turned and took a drink of his coffee. "Go ahead, poke fun. Just remember that you're both going to find mates sooner or later, and I won't forget this."

Cade grinned. "We wouldn't have it any other way." He sobered and set his mug down on the counter. "Any regrets?"

"Not with mating Simon. Wish it hadn't happened because he was dying. Would have liked a little more time. But no, no regrets."

"Good." Liam thumped Gray on the back. "You have our support. We'll get through this."

"Agreed," Cade added.

"I'm putting in a call to the Were Council this morning, but my priority is getting the security system updated."

At the mention of the security system, Cade's thoughts turned to the previous night and his confrontation with Rocky that had turned into... what? Rocky had been just as turned on as Cade, but something about the other wolf had rubbed Cade wrong from the first time they'd met. He'd walked away before things got too hot and heavy, even though it had been difficult.

"What?" Gray asked.

"How much do we know about Rocky?"

"Not much. I asked for a recommendation and found out about Rocky's company. His alpha gave him permission to be here. You suspect something?"

"No. It's not that. The guy knows his business." Cade shrugged. "I just... get a bad vibe or something."

"Cade?"

He'd never been able to lie to Gray. "It's nothing, really. Last night, I had a little run-in with him. We worked it out, but it got me thinking about how little we know. With everything going on, having an outsider around might not be smart."

Liam agreed. "Good point."

Gray nodded. "What's your schedule like this week?"

"I'm not busy. Have a few little things, but nothing I can't put off. Unless there's an emergency or something. Plus extra patrols."

"Okay. Let me know if there's an emergency. Otherwise, I want you helping Rocky. Keep an eye out, and if you have any other suspicions, let me know."

"Will do."

Liam turned his head to the side. "Someone's coming."

Gray listened as well.

Cade sniffed the air and inhaled the familiar scent of their security specialist. "It's Rocky."

. . .

Simon settled on the grass in the backyard to do his morning meditation. He usually meditated prior to doing anything else, but between making breakfast and their morning sex talk with Garon, he hadn't had a chance to get outside before now. His entire schedule felt off, but it was still early enough in the day that he could enjoy the stability his morning meditation gave him.

Cade and Liam's early arrival had thrown him off as well. The easy camaraderie between the three friends left Simon feeling out of place. He'd excused himself as quickly as he could. One more thing on the list he needed to understand about the were-culture he'd committed himself to. More than his morning routine would have to change if he continued living with Gray and the pack.

If. The word stuck in Simon's mind even as he shifted on the grass to get comfortable. The blades of grass tickled the backs of his legs through his pajama pants, and Simon tried to focus on that sensation instead. *If.*

The morning breeze cooled his overheated face. The few puffy white clouds that floated high above him in the sky didn't keep the sun from shining directly on the little patch of yard where he sat. Simon closed his eyes and let his head fall back. Little dots of black and yellow floated across his eyelids.

They were mated. Period. Simon couldn't exactly change his mind. Not that he wanted to. It was just so crazy. He'd only known the wolves for a few weeks, and now he had a mate? What did that even mean? And a what? Stepson? Is that what Garon was to him? He'd gone from being an apprentice mage who lived an isolated life while training, to a… hell, Simon didn't even know what to call himself right now.

He tried to center himself. The magic inside him churned wildly, echoing his frantic thoughts. He attempted to corral it, pulling the random threads together inside him until his control returned. *If.* What if it wasn't just him feeling this crazy rush of doubts? What if Gray had doubts of his own?

Simon shook his head and forced the negative energy away. Instead, he concentrated on his power. It crackled from his fingertips, sparks of brilliantly colored blues and greens. He'd never had this much magic at hand before. The sensations were nearly as overwhelming as his doubts over his relationship with Gray.

Simon really didn't understand why the alpha wolf had wanted to mate him. Was it really just because he'd saved Garon? It wasn't enough of a reason to commit to spending the rest of their lives together.

His feckless attempts at control caused his magic to roil around inside him. Simon closed his eyes and targeted the curving lines around him. He cornered them and pulled the static charges back into his body. It finally began to work. Simon let out a breath and focused on the power.

The morning conversation with Garon drifted back to the forefront of his mind. Garon wasn't an issue. From the moment he'd seen the boy standing protectively in front of the other kids when the demon held them captive, Simon had known there was something special about Garon.

And there really wasn't an issue with Gray either.

Change. Simon hated it and had never dealt with it well. With all the upheaval of the past few weeks, Simon needed time to wrap his brain around everything. He had to find a way to accept his new life and his new powers.

In a way, it reminded him of his garden. The seeds he planted nestled in the ground until it rained or he watered them by hand. They took root, nourished by the soil and water. His magic was like that before Thomas siphoned part of his energy. Now his "garden" resembled one that hadn't been tended for months. Simon needed to make the rows neat and tidy so he could flourish.

And he only had a week to do it. Turning twenty-five held so much significance to the mages. Simon wondered what exactly would happen to him on that day. Cormac could probably tell him, but his vampire relative was sleeping the day away in the upstairs guest room.

Simon smiled at the thought. Who knew Gray would suddenly end up with a mage for a mate and a vampire for a, what, great-grandfa-ther-in-law? The more Simon thought about it, the more he began to shake with laughter. After a minute he was laughing so hard he couldn't breathe. A sudden shout from behind him startled him so much he snorted and doubled over again.

"Simon!"

Simon wiped his eyes and turned to see what Garon needed. He looked down. *Way down.* He floated in the air about twenty feet off the ground. *Holy shit.* How the hell had he managed to do that?

Garon stared up at him with a terrified expression on his face. The look of fear immediately sobered Simon, and he began to try to think of a way to get down to the ground again. As he calmed, his magic provided the answer, and he dropped quickly to the ground. Landing on his ass, Simon grunted in pain before collapsing onto his back.

4

*R*ocky stood on the front porch of Gray's house, the debate in his mind over whether or not to knock going strong. Crossing this line, offering reparation on his alpha's command, would be the point of no return. He'd given his alpha information before, but actively helping him get inside a pack? He'd never had to go that far.

Either way, he owed the alpha an apology for his crass attitude toward the man who was now the alpha-mate. From the moment he'd met Simon, Rocky had put up a shield of wariness and distrust. Although his intentions hadn't been altogether wrong, Rocky should at least have given Simon a chance. He deserved that much.

That was the easy apology. The tough one required admitting he'd failed Gray the night before. Rocky hated to admit failure. When Malone told him to volunteer to go with the pack to rescue Simon, he thought there would be some posturing, maybe some yelling and demands made on Gray's part. The reality of the fight that took place? It was the stuff of nightmares. There was no way to prepare for a mage willing to slice his own apprentice into shreds and drain him of his magic.

Even if Malone hadn't commanded him to take this step, Rocky would have been driven to do so anyway. He had failed Gray, and although this was supposed to make amends for that, by allowing Malone to manipulate the situation, Rocky was adding more fuel to the fire.

If he didn't go ahead and get the apology over with, he'd just head back to his cabin and live with this gut-churning guilt. That would make him a coward, and Rocky would be damned before he let himself give in to that emotion.

He straightened his spine and rapped sharply on the door. From inside, Garon yelled, "I'll get it." He heard the sound of feet running toward the door, and then it flew open.

"Hey, Rocky." Garon smiled. "My dad's in the kitchen."

Rocky stepped inside, and Garon shut the door behind him.

"Dad, Rocky's here."

Rocky winced at the volume. His nerves sent warning flutters to his stomach.

Gray walked out of the kitchen. "Morning, Rocky."

"Alpha Gray. Do you have a few minutes?"

"Sure. Come on in."

Rocky followed Gray through the house and into the kitchen.

"Hey, Dad, can I go outside with Simon?"

"Go ahead. But stay in the yard. And don't bother him."

"I won't. Bye, everybody!" Garon took off at a run, and the back door slammed behind him.

Cade and Liam looked up from where they sat on stools at the counter. The alpha poured himself a mug of coffee. He offered one to Rocky, but he declined. He didn't think his stomach could handle the addition of the bitter brew.

"Sorry, I didn't know you were busy. I should have called first."

"Not a problem. What can I do for you?"

Rocky's mouth went dry. "I needed to speak with you for a moment." He looked away from the alpha, but his gaze caught on Cade.

Cade stared at Rocky for a long moment. The other wolf seemed to sense his nervousness. "Actually, Liam and I need to get going. We'll catch up with you later, Gray."

The two left the kitchen, leaving Rocky alone to face his confession.

Gray took a large gulp of coffee and sighed. "I haven't had enough caffeine yet this morning. You'll have to bear with me."

Rocky shook his head and laughed. Gray's easy way helped his discomfort. "Everything okay after last night?"

"Honestly, we'll have to wait and see. I'll notify the Were Council. They'll no doubt send a representative to meet with us. You'll be included in that, of course, as one of the wolves present at the time."

Rocky looked down at his hands, unable to hold Gray's gaze any longer. "About that…"

When he told Gray his presence would help with any questions the alpha's actions raised with the Were Council, he'd meant it. But his motives hadn't been entirely pure. Some part of him wanted to be there to witness the showdown between the High Moon Pack Alpha and the mages. The confrontation should have been one for the history books. A wolf pack versus the Mage Conclave. To Rocky's knowledge, nothing like that had ever happened before. If it had, it wasn't in any of the history books he'd read. Rocky had been thinking of that when he'd tried to get added to the team, not how his presence would help them get Simon back.

He would be able to corroborate Gray's version of the story as an outside source. And with the way things had gone down, Gray was going to need all the backup he could get. The big argument he'd been expecting with the mages had just been a battle with one crazy mage with ulterior motives of his own. Rocky had stood in the shadows, shocked by the rush of complete terror he'd experienced. Thomas, the mage who'd attacked Simon, threw a barrage of spells at the wolves that stopped the pack members in their tracks.

"Rocky? What's going on?"

"I owe you an apology." Rocky paused and let out a long breath. "No, more than an apology. My actions last night during the fight were unforgivable."

Gray leaned back against the counter and set his mug beside him. "I think you need to explain yourself."

"I froze, Alpha. Your mate was in danger—hell, *you* were in danger —and I fucking froze. I didn't do a damn thing to help. I saw Cade and Liam thrown around like toys, and that vampire just tore through everything, throwing spells and getting knocked back. And I didn't do a damn thing."

If Cormac hadn't been there, Rocky didn't think any of them would have made it out alive. The first vampire Rocky had ever met, Cormac's countenance was more of a young scholar. What an illusion that turned out to be. Cormac had fought and killed the mage, all while Rocky hid like a scared pup. An overwhelming sense of shame consumed him, and both his man and wolf sides agreed that he owed Gray more than just an apology.

Actually doing it, though, offering himself to Gray for whatever punishment the alpha saw fit, went against the man he showed to the outside world. If he did this, Gray would know his secret, and it could bring his carefully structured world falling down around him.

Rocky hadn't been with the pack during their last full moon, but when he shifted the night before during his confrontation with Cade, he'd let the wolf out of the bag. In less than thirty seconds, Cade had taken him down. If the alpha's best friend took any time to think it through, he would realize Rocky was an omega.

But he wouldn't be the man, or wolf, he wanted to be if he let his weakness define him.

"At the next full moon, I'd like to make reparations to you and your mate."

When Gray didn't respond, Rocky dared to raise his eyes. Gray stared across the kitchen at him, his expression blank. "As you aren't a member of the High Moon Pack, I can't accept reparation without discussing it with your alpha. On the one hand, you agreed to go along as a witness, and you did what you agreed to do. But Rocky, you know you'd never stand by and watch another wolf in danger and do nothing."

Rocky had never heard Gray's voice so low and dark. Directed at him? Another rush of humiliation at his weakness gnawed at the core of him. Rocky leaned forward with his elbows on his knees and dropped his head into his hands. "I know. Call Alpha Malone. You're right."

Weak. The description haunted him. He'd fought as a man to make himself as strong as possible. He learned to fight and to win, using his fists and any other body part he could to make sure he could take care of himself.

But as a wolf, weak defined him. His other side didn't stand a chance around most others of his kind. Most packs wouldn't even allow an omega into their ranks. Rocky's entire family had been shunned for their status for most of his life.

When they'd finally been allowed to join a pack, it wasn't every-thing his family had dreamed of. They were the bottom of the barrel, the lowest of the low. By that point, his family didn't care; they just wanted to belong. Rocky minded, though, and set out to prove every day that he wasn't beneath any of them.

He couldn't think about his family now or his bitterness and resentment would be clear for Gray to see. Besides, he'd done the same thing to the alpha-mate.

"Alpha Gray, I'd also like to apologize to your mate, if he's available."

Gray gave him a brief nod in reply. "Let's go outside."

Garon gave a frightened yell from the backyard. Gray dropped his mug and took off running. Rocky ran after him, determined to redeem himself with this alpha, whatever the cost.

Garon rushed over to Simon's side and dropped to his knees. "Are you okay? Do I need to call Dad?"

"Nope," Simon chuckled. "I'm fine." He patted the ground beside him, and Garon sat down in the grass.

"Are you sure? Because I've never seen anyone do that before. And you fell really fast."

Gray leapt over the railing and ran to Simon's side. "What happened? Are you hurt?"

Simon took quick inventory of his body and realized that, other than a bit of a sore rear end, nothing hurt.

"Nothing's hurt. I promise."

Gray and Garon let out sighs of relief. "Simon, were you flying?"

Simon held out his hand, and Gray helped him sit up. He winced when all his weight pressed onto his bruised ass.

"Nope. I'm honestly not sure what exactly I was doing, but I wouldn't call it flying. Floating, maybe."

"Weird. You were really high!"

Gray's voice appeared in his mind through their link. *Define "really high."*

Simon grinned and patted his arm. *I'll tell you later. I don't want to worry Garon.* "No kidding. You were really short from way up there." Simon grabbed Garon's knee and gave it a little squeeze.

Garon jerked away with a laugh. "That tickles!"

Gray cleared his throat, and they both looked up at him. "Simon, I need to speak to you for a minute."

"Uh-oh, that's his 'you're in trouble' voice."

Simon tickled Garon again. "I'm not in trouble. You're in trouble."

"Nuh-uh. I didn't fly, you did!"

"Yeah, yeah. Okay, you hang out here for a few minutes. I'm going to talk to your dad."

Gray reached out his hand to Simon and pulled him to his feet. He wrapped an arm around Simon's shoulder and tucked him into his side. Simon looked up at him with a puzzled frown.

"What's wrong?"

"Everything's fine. Rocky has something he'd like to say to you."

Simon turned to face Rocky. The visiting wolf looked troubled, his face pale and lined with tension.

"Simon, I wanted to apologize for the way I've been treating you. I've never been around a mage before, and, well, it's no excuse for my rudeness. I wish I'd helped last night. I apologized to Gray for that, but I'd like to apologize to you also."

"It's o—"

Gray squeezed Simon against him, which cut him off midword. "It's not okay. We accept your apology, Rocky."

Simon glared up at Gray. His mate stared back, his stern glance enough to keep Simon quiet. After a moment, Gray broke the staring match with Simon and looked over at Rocky.

"Thank you, Alpha. And Alpha-mate."

"Okay, go on and get to work. I know you have some things to do on the security system today. I'll make the call as soon as I can. You'll either hear from your alpha or myself later on."

"Thank you, Alpha. And I'll get you an update as soon as I have one."

As soon as Rocky left the yard, Simon spun around and faced Gray. "Why did you cut me off?"

"It's part of our culture, Simon. It's important for you to accept an apology, not simply brush it off."

Simon grumbled. "Yet another thing I don't understand."

"Hey." Gray tilted Simon's face up and pressed a quick kiss to his lips. "I don't expect you to know everything. Come on. Give yourself a break. I'll help you, okay?"

Simon nodded.

"I'm going to go call the Council and Rocky's alpha."

"I'm going to hang out with Garon for a few, then take a quick shower."

Gray leaned in and kissed Simon again. "Please be careful."

"Always."

Gray went back inside, and Simon turned to find Garon staring at him. The boy looked worried. Simon crouched down beside him and tousled Garon's hair.

"Simon, am I going to fly like that? What if I float away or something?"

5

*S*imon sat down on the grass and wrapped an arm around Garon's shoulder. "Hey, you aren't going to have to worry about floating away. You have me and Cormac to make sure you know everything you need to. Now, I don't know exactly what happened, but I'm sure Cormac can explain it. We'll have to talk to him when he gets up."

"That would be good. I know everyone thinks it's weird that I can do stuff like you."

"Well, I don't think it's weird at all. I think it's pretty cool. I was thinking that maybe we could talk to your dad about both of us working with Cormac a little. What do you think? A little magic school? We can work on plants together, and then Cormac can help us with this other stuff."

Garon nodded. "I think that would be cool. But, uh, it won't really be school will it?"

"I don't know. We'll have to ask Cormac."

"Okay, as long as I don't have to do homework or anything."

Simon laughed and lay down on his back. "Let's talk to your dad first and make sure he's okay with it."

"Yeah." Garon stretched out beside Simon, and they stared up at the clear morning sky. "If I get grass stains on my clothes, Aunt Maggie is going to make me scrub them."

"Me too. I guess we'll scrub 'em together."

Garon knocked his arm into Simon's. "I'm glad you're going to stay with us, Simon. We're going to have fun. And Dad really likes you."

Those *ifs* that had been floating around in Simon's mind suddenly eased. He glanced over at Garon and saw the sincerity in his gaze. "I like you guys too."

Garon nodded back in a way that made him seem much older, as if he understood the worries that weighed Simon down, and instinctively knew how to soothe them. They stared back up at the sky for a long moment, the rustling of the leaves the only sounds breaking up the quiet.

"Hey, Simon. Look. It's a wolf!" Garon pointed up to the clouds overhead.

Simon followed Garon's finger, and sure enough, one of the floating clouds resembled a wolf. Maybe it was a sign he was where he was supposed to be.

They trudged back inside after a few minutes and found Aunt Maggie waiting for them. Simon and Garon made a production of checking their clothes for stains to make her laugh. She shooed them both off when they'd convinced her they were innocent of all stain charges, and Simon went to shower. He tossed his thankfully unstained pajama bottoms into the hamper. He didn't plan on letting Maggie do his laundry, but if she got to them before he did, he didn't want her to have any extra work.

He and Gray really needed to talk through some of this stuff. Simon's doubts from earlier began to creep back in, but he pushed them aside with a determined shove. Until Gray answered some of his questions, he couldn't let his worries fester. After turning on the shower to let the water warm up, Simon stripped off his boxers and climbed into the shower. The hot water started to ease his tension. He sighed as he let his head fall forward so the tight muscles of his neck could get some relief.

A cool draft alerted him to someone opening the bathroom door, and he peeked around the curtain to find Gray stripping off his clothes with a sparkle in his eyes. Simon rolled his eyes and closed the curtain before Gray could see his grin.

He rubbed his blackberry and sage soap between his hands, then placed it back on the shelf beside Gray's bottle of bodywash. The sight of his stuff sitting there right next to Gray's had him shaking his head with a puzzled frown. Simon wondered how long it was going to take for him to get used to all the changes in his life, when even the little things like having more than one kind of soap in the shower threw him for a loop.

Gray stepped into the shower behind Simon and pulled the curtain closed. He grabbed Simon by the hips and pulled him in close. Simon relaxed his body against his mate and rubbed his back against the hair on Gray's chest. Gray nipped him on the ear before nuzzling his face into Simon's neck.

"Mmm. Your soap smells good. I think that's my new favorite scent."

Simon ran his sudsy hands down Gray's arms and covered Gray's hands where they rested at his stomach. "I'll make more."

"Yeah. You do that. You going to tell me how high you were to make Garon yell like that?"

Gray ran his hands down Simon's ribs and over his hips before sneaking farther down Simon's front to give his dick a quick stroke.

Simon's blood rushed south, and his cock began to lengthen in Gray's hand. "Not if you keep doing that."

Gray chuckled and gave him another stroke. Simon's body perked up even more.

"Just tell me if I need to be worried."

"No, nothing to worry about. Oh God, unless you stop doing that." He thrust his hips forward, and Gray fisted his dick as it hardened.

"I want to fuck you, right here in the shower."

"So I gathered." Simon looked over his shoulder with a little smirk and laid his head back against Gray's shoulder.

"I'm an alpha, you know. I have needs."

Simon burst out laughing at the reminder of Garon's earlier

comments. Gray chuckled as well, his shaking body sending answering tremors through Simon. "That was the most terrifying conversation I've ever had in my life," Simon said once their laughter faded.

"You scared me half to death when you called me this morning. Then I walked in the kitchen to hear my kid asking you about sex, and I about keeled over again. Man, I thought I had a while to wait for those talks, but he's growing up fast on me."

Simon spun around in Gray's arms and laid his hands on Gray's broad shoulders. "There's a lot of changes lately. I'm sure he's just confused."

Gray cupped Simon's jaw in his hand and pressed a gentle kiss to his lips. "He's not the only one."

"Yeah?"

"We'll work it out. Keep getting to know each other. We'll probably fight some, but hey, that'll just mean make-up sex."

Simon ran a hand around Gray's neck and brushed his fingers through Gray's damp hair. "At least we know the sex isn't a problem."

"Even if it was, we'd work it out. Promise me, Simon. If we have problems, we work them out. Together."

Simon stared into Gray's eyes for a long moment, then kissed the corner of his mouth. "I promise," he whispered.

"Now, how about taking care of those needs of mine?"

"Pfft. I think you should take care of me."

Gray spun Simon around and pressed him up against the tiled wall. "That can be arranged."

The steamy water ran over them both, slicking their skin as it raced down their shoulders and backs. Simon braced his hands against the wall and spread his legs to allow Gray more room. His mate took advantage of the position and pressed his cock into the crease of Simon's ass. Simon arched his back and pushed himself against the thick length teasing him.

Gray fumbled around in the plastic basket of supplies hanging on the wall and fished out a little tube of waterproof lube. "Thank God," he mumbled as he flipped it open and poured the slick over his cock.

He rubbed it over his length, then guided himself into Simon's opening.

Simon pushed back and groaned as Gray's thickness penetrated him. That first stretch was both the best and the worst part. He could feel the ridges of the head as it pushed through his hole. A burst of pleasure rushed through Simon when Gray's cock brushed against the nub inside him.

Gray grabbed Simon's hips and held him steady until his body began to relax. When he gave Gray the signal that he was ready, Gray began to thrust, slowly at first, teasing his way in and out. Simon arched his back and turned his head enough to meet Gray's eyes. He moaned when the quick change of angle caused Gray's cock to pound him right where he needed it most. "Right there, Gray. Oh God."

His knees grew weak, and he leaned his head against Gray's shoulder. Gray wrapped one arm around Simon's waist and held onto his leg with the other. His thrusts were more shallow this way, but they felt so damn good. The short jabs continued to batter Simon's gland. With his whole body sensitized from their marathon session the previous night, it didn't take long before Simon's orgasm pulsed through him. He keened as his balls drew up, and he came all over the shower wall. Gray stilled behind him for just a minute, waited until Simon unclenched his ass enough for him to thrust a few more times, then he flooded Simon's hole with his release.

They both breathed in fast gulps as they came down from the rush of pleasure. Simon shivered when Gray's softening cock slid from his body, and he turned on shaky legs to wrap his arms around Gray's broad chest.

The hot water from the shower pounded down on his back, and Gray reached behind Simon to sluice the water over his entrance to help clean him up. After another quick wash with the shower gel, they stepped out of the shower and dried off. Gray wrapped his towel around his waist and leaned against the counter to watch Simon dress.

"Shame to cover up all that lickable skin," he mumbled when Simon pulled on his boxers.

"So you want everyone to see it?"

Gray arched a brow and pretended to scowl. "Mine."

"Yeah, yeah."

His faded jeans went on next, followed by one of his favorite T-shirts. Gray snorted when Simon smoothed it over his chest.

"What?"

"I'm a fungi?"

Simon glanced down at the orange and brown mushroom covering the front of his chest. "What? You don't think I'm fun?" He glanced over at the shower and back at his mate.

"Well, I guess you have a point."

"Of course I do."

Simon ran a comb through his hair and watched in the mirror as Gray pulled on his faded jeans. He'd have to find Gray something fun to wear for Christmas. He laughed to himself when he realized he was already thinking about being here so many months ahead.

"We're having a pack meeting later so I can formally introduce you to the pack."

Simon spun around and stared. "A what?"

Gray rubbed the towel over his chest to get a little more moisture out of his chest hair. He glanced up when Simon spoke. "A pack meeting."

"For the whole pack?"

"Uh, yeah? Why?"

"Do we have to?" For some reason, the idea of facing the entire pack terrified Simon.

"Yes."

"Why?"

Gray tossed the towel onto the counter and pulled Simon close. "Because I want to make it official. I want to tell them I've taken a mate and give them a chance to celebrate with us."

"Are you sure they'll celebrate?"

"I'm sure. And if they don't, well, we'll deal with that as it comes. You worry too much."

Simon agreed that he probably did, but then again, lately he seemed to have lots of things to worry about.

Rocky walked out of Gray's house barely able to breathe. Simon could, what, fly? Float? Whatever the hell he'd been doing. And he wasn't even into his full powers yet? It would only get worse as he got stronger. What sort of control could he get over the pack?

Then again, Gray planned to follow the process and report everything to the Were Council. Surely they'd intervene? If nothing else, the fact that the mind-link worked between them gave Rocky some idea that he'd judged too harshly. If the magic allowed them to communicate like the pack did, maybe it wasn't wrong? Rocky couldn't wrap his mind around it. Everything he'd ever been taught claimed the opposite.

He grabbed his phone from the carrier clipped to his shorts. Malone would want an update. But what to say? How much deeper did he want to dig himself?

The low rumbling of a vehicle growing closer drew Rocky out of his thoughts. He closed the phone and put it away. A large white pickup truck approached from the parking area of the compound. Its tires spat small pieces of gravel from beneath them, even though the truck wasn't going fast. Rocky paused at the turnoff that led to the alpha's house and waited for it to pass before he continued on to his cabin to pick up the supplies he needed.

He looked up when the truck stopped beside him to see Cade behind the wheel. Cade lowered the window and laid one muscled arm across the opening. "Need a lift?"

Remembering the strength in Cade's body from their brief training session the night before sent a rush of heat through Rocky. He considered himself to be in great shape. Hours of working out kept his body long and lean. He'd never have the bulk some guys had, but his training made him more agile than bigger guys. Guys like Cade, whose thick, brawny muscles Rocky lusted over. The man's chest must have been molded from hours of bodybuilding, intense lifting to get that perfect, sculpted marble form. His skin was a deep, luscious brown, and the dark tone enhanced every chiseled muscle. Cade's body exuded power, much like many of the alphas Rocky had met. And most of those were men Rocky needed to avoid.

"Nah, just going down to my cabin." Rocky thought he'd gotten out of spending that little bit of time with Cade, but Cade didn't take the hint.

Cade rapped his hand against the door with a grin. "Well, go on and climb in, and I'll take you down there."

"I—"

"Rocky, don't argue about everything, man. Just get in the truck."

The exasperated expression on Cade's face was enough to make Rocky pause and reconsider. "You've got my number, don't you?" Rocky asked.

Cade shook his head and grinned. "Yeah. I think I've got you figured out, about some things at least." His expression changed, and his smile dimmed a little. "In others? Not so much."

Rocky crossed in front of the truck and climbed into the passenger side. "So, about last night. Sorry I was such an ass."

Cade shrugged and drove the truck down to the gravel area they used for parking. "It happens. I was serious about you showing me how to do some of those martial arts moves."

"No problem. And you'll show me how you shifted so fast?"

"If I can."

They got out of the truck, and Cade followed Rocky up the path toward their cabins. Cade lived a little past the one Rocky was using, so he'd have company for his entire walk. He decided to try to be a little more sociable and maybe mend the bridge a bit.

"You, Gray, and Liam seem really close. Guess you guys have been friends a long time."

"We grew up together here in the pack. The only time we've been apart is when Gray and Liam went off to college."

"You didn't go with them?"

"Nah. I didn't get along with school very well. Did what I had to do to graduate and went on to a trade school."

44

"You take care of everything around here, don't you? Repairs and stuff?"

"That's me. Handyman Cade."

Cade didn't seem to want to discuss it further. Rocky was at a loss as to how to keep up the small talk. They reached the path that led to Rocky's cabin, and he veered off to the right. "Well, I'll catch you later. I'm going to work on installing some motion sensors today."

"Hey, Rocky, wait."

Rocky stopped and turned to meet Cade's gaze. "Yeah?"

"Need a hand?"

For a moment, Rocky considered rejecting Cade's offer outright. He didn't need the added complication of making friends here who would become enemies when they found out what he'd done.

Instead, he searched Cade's face for any signs of, well, anything really. He wasn't sure what he expected to find, but there wasn't anything in Cade's expression besides that simple question. Nothing more than an honest offer of help. "Sure, if you aren't busy."

Cade nodded and followed Rocky back to his cabin. He gathered the tools and supplies he needed while Cade stood by and watched. Cade did that a lot. Just watched. Rocky figured he knew more about what went on in his pack than folks gave him credit for. Liam might be the official beta, but Gray really had a second one in Cade.

They worked in companionable silence for several hours, installing the equipment in strategic areas around the compound. Cade stayed quiet for the most part, which Rocky appreciated. There were a few moments of tenseness that he couldn't quite identify, a look or two that he couldn't explain, but in the end, Rocky wrote them off as oddities and went on with his day.

ade hovered near the back of the meeting hall and watched as the pack gathered for Gray's big announcement. They all knew already; the alpha couldn't keep secrets from his pack. Especially not one as big as taking a mate. He was the center of their world. This meeting was more a formality. Gray needed to officially introduce Simon as his mate.

The aged wooden walls of the room told the tale of their pack. A few years before, Cade had rewired the large lantern-like lights to the thick beams that stretched the entire length of the ceiling. During the holiday months, he strung holly swags and strings of white lights from one end to the other. This building represented them and symbolized home in many ways. Since it had been built in the early 1920s, it had become the gathering place for the pack, a place where a helpful hand or friendly ear could generally be found.

Cade's gaze drifted from the faded black-and-white photographs of their former alphas that lined one long wall to the front of the room where Gray stood with Simon, Garon, and Liam at his side. Their future. Cade could tell Simon's nerves were getting the better of him. The alpha-mate rocked anxiously from side to side and plucked at the buttons on his button-down black shirt. Cade met Simon's gaze and gave him a reassuring smile.

Maggie slipped in through the side door. Cade winked at her, and she walked over to his side. Her long gray hair hung loose down her back, and a swishy purple skirt swung down to her ankles. "Simon looks nervous," she whispered.

"Yeah. He doesn't know enough about our ways yet to know he shouldn't do that. Where's Cormac? He usually helps Simon stay calm."

Maggie sighed. "He left as soon as it got dark. Apparently he didn't think it would be a good idea to be in a room with an entire pack of wolves."

Cade glanced back at Simon. Gray had pulled him closer, and Simon ceased his nervous twitching. Good. He needed to keep it together. Turning his attention back to Maggie, Cade winked at her. "You look really nice, by the way."

"Oh, quit your flirting. It won't get you anywhere."

Cade dropped his arm around her shoulders as more of the pack came in and sat at the long tables that filled the center of the room. Parents corralled their cubs, and once everyone settled, Gray stepped forward and held up a hand for silence.

They all straightened up and turned their attention to him.

Gray smiled and opened his arms wide to his sides. He gave a push of power that soared through the pack, and several of them howled out their pleasure at the surge. Cade and Maggie added theirs to the mix. Their alpha's strength filled them to excess, satiated their need for security and stability in the midst of their evolution as a pack.

"High Moon Pack, just over four years ago, I completed the training of my father and his before him to become your alpha. In that time, we have grown as a pack, both in our numbers and in our might. Today I announce to you that I have taken Simon Osbourne, Apprentice Mage of the Earthhaven Mages as my mate. With the alpha-mate by my side, the High Moon Pack will continue to flourish. Welcome him to our family!"

A symphony of howls burst forth from the pack. Cade lent his to the chorus, his deep bass echoing through the large room. He noticed the nervous glances a few of the pack members shared and made a list of potential troublemakers.

"It is a time of celebration. My mate will have his twenty-fifth birthday in a week, and at that time we will host a party to honor this milestone, as well as our union. Everyone, please join us in commemorating both of these occasions."

"Yay, Simon!" Everyone chuckled when Emma stood up in her chair and cheered. Her mom tried to shush her and get her to sit back down, but by that point the mood had turned festive, and everyone stood up and surged to the front of the room to offer Gray and Simon their congratulations.

Cade hung back and watched. He made note of the few mumbled words of disapproval from the stragglers, but even they went up to greet Gray and Simon. Cade had high hopes that everything would settle once the pack got to know Simon better.

When the pack began filling their plates from the potluck buffet set up along the side wall, Cade hurried over to get in line. He could smell his favorite cucumber dip a mile away. Aunt Maggie didn't make it very often, and Cade had never been able to recreate it no matter how many times he tried or how many recipes he looked up.

She'd made a big bowl this time and surrounded it with crunchy pita chips. Cade ignored the piles of meatballs and sliced vegetables and made his way to the *tzatziki* goodness. Maggie stepped behind the table and gave him a warning glare. *One time*, he thought. Only once, and she still hadn't forgiven him. And it had been fifteen years ago. All he'd done was take the whole tray, bowl and all, to his table. He hadn't even double dipped.

Cade smothered a smile as he spooned out an extra-large portion and added a stack of pita chips to his otherwise empty plate. He waggled his eyebrows at Maggie before adding a single carrot stick and a meatball to his plate. She finally lost it and cackled as he made his way back to an empty seat.

Liam joined him after getting a plate of his own. "That went well."

"Yeah," Cade replied. "I didn't expect any less. There are some doubters in the bunch, but that would happen no matter what. You know how protective everyone is of Gray and Garon."

It was true. The entire pack adored their alpha and his son. Cade figured it would take them a little time to warm up to Simon, to make sure he was "good enough" for their leader. The way he'd saved Garon, not once but twice, had made a huge dent in the negativity. It was hard to hate someone who'd saved their cubs from certain death at the hands of a deranged demon.

Besides, it wasn't in their nature to hate anyway. Cade remembered his parents talking about joining the pack. Back then, it wasn't kosher for couples to mix races, even among the weres. Bigotry was alive and well in the South, but when his parents mated, they found a home with the High Moon Pack.

It was funny, really. Cade's dad was a doctor, his mother a nurse. Their contributions to any pack should have been welcomed with open arms. Having a doctor on hand was a gift to the pack, a skill that most couldn't provide. Other packs had turned them away, but they settled here with no problems. Geoffrey Townsend, Gray's father, didn't put up with any bullshit on his watch.

The pack had lost three skilled members when Cade's parents decided to move to his brother-in-law's pack after his older sister mated and began having little ones. They maintained their official status as members here but were "permanent guests" with the Pokagon Pack in northern Indiana. Cade's parents visited him several times a year, and he went up to see them on major holidays. Sometimes the seven-hour drive that separated them felt too long, but his nieces needed their grandparents around. Cade respected that.

As much as he missed his family, his bond with this pack grew stronger every day. Cade would never leave Gray. He respected the hell out of his best friend and knew his place was guarding Gray's back. Looking around the room, he decided that he'd do some quick talking to the few who were worried about Simon. It was the least he could do.

Cade noticed Rocky across the rec hall. His faded jeans fit him like a glove, cupping his ass and making his legs seem long and lean. Cade gulped down part of his drink. Rocky looked around the room when he finished filling his plate. Cade waved him over. Liam smirked, and Cade kicked him under the table. "Shut up."

"I didn't say anything. But I find it amusing that you get that stupid grin every time you see him."

"What? I don't get a stupid grin. He annoys the shit out of me most of the time. He's a guest, though, so we have to make him feel welcome."

"Sure, buddy. It's your story. Tell it like you want it."

Rocky sat down across the table from Cade, and Liam turned his attention to his full plate. Rocky looked over at Cade's pile of chips and raised a questioning brow.

"I like the dip."

"So I see," Rocky chuckled. His plate held a big pile of fruit and vegetables. Cade reached over and snagged a celery stick and dunked it into his *tzatziki*. "Hey, hands off my plate."

Cade grinned and stuck the celery into his mouth. Instead of biting off a piece, he slurped the *tzatziki* off. Rocky's eyes widened, and a flush crept up his neck. Cade's heart rate began to pick up. He hadn't intended the move to be sexual, but now that he thought about it, he'd given a pretty damn fine example of how much he liked to suck.

He wasn't really into Rocky like that, though. Was he? Rocky's body could induce wet dreams in the straightest of men, and Cade didn't qualify for that list. He'd always been more of an equal opportunity lover. Chemistry sizzled between them, on a physical level at least. Personality wise? Rocky could be damn irritating.

Rocky tore his gaze away from Cade's mouth and turned his attention to his own food. Cade watched him chomp down on a meatball. A drop of deep red sauce clung to his lips. Rocky swiped his tongue over it. Cade had to swallow a groan. Rocky didn't notice. He swirled a carrot stick into a dab of dip much more reasonable than the one on Cade's plate.

Cade forced his gaze away before the vegetable in question made it to Rocky's mouth. No way could he make it through seeing his favorite dip disappearing into Rocky's mouth without wanting a taste from the source. He turned to Liam for distraction and found his friend fighting back laughter. His gaze drifted back and forth between Cade and Rocky while he happily devoured his own food.

Cade sent another well-placed kick to his shin under the table. Liam choked and coughed a few times, but Cade ignored him. Rocky watched a moment and, when Liam finally quit coughing, asked if he was okay.

"Oh yeah. I'm fine. Just went down the wrong way." Liam glared at Cade for a moment before taking a long drink of water. When he swallowed, he glanced between Cade and Rocky again, then excused himself from the table. "I'm going to go make sure Gray and Simon get something to eat. They're still surrounded."

Cade shook his head at the lame excuse. There was no way Gray and Simon wouldn't have already received plates full of food from someone. But Liam's exit left them alone at the table, and Cade used the opportunity to meet Rocky's eyes again. "So how's everything going?"

"Good. I wish I'd been able to bring in more of my team to help get stuff done, but we had a lot of jobs lined up."

"You don't seem to be as pissed off as you were."

Rocky shrugged and stuffed his mouth full. Cade sat and stared until he finished chewing. "Well, I'm still uncomfortable, and there's a lot going on that I'm not sure about, but being taken down by you the other night seemed to knock some of the chip off my shoulder."

"I don't really know what's making you so uncomfortable, especially now that you've met Simon, but I'm glad it's easing up."

Rocky looked over at Gray and Simon then back at Cade. "An alpha is only as strong as his mate."

"I know," Cade answered as he stood up to go sneak another round of dip from the table. "Gray is a lucky man."

Before Cade could get far, the low sound of a guitar being strummed began to drift through the room. Cade searched the room, finally locating Roger in the front corner. He sat casually on a stool, his instrument laid across his lap as he plucked out the final chords of his tuning process.

The hum of voices softened, and smiles started to form on everyone's faces. Cade saw Simon glancing around in confusion, but that look faded as Roger's voice drifted out, low and husky. Gray dropped his arm across Simon's shoulders and pulled him close. Pack members began to pull up chairs, and the kids scrambled to find seats at the musician's feet.

After the first verse, Gray led Simon forward, and they swayed together in time with the music. The melody began to build, and Roger's voice grew stronger. All other noises in the room faded into the background. Cade sat back down, watching Simon and Gray drifting back and forth in each other's arms. Gray rested his cheek against Simon's, and the sheer strength of the alpha's feelings for his mate showed on his face.

Cade didn't think he was the only one who noticed. He glanced around at the rest of the pack, and they were all as captivated by Gray and Simon as he was. As Roger's voice grew louder at the climax of the song, Gray pulled Simon more tightly against him. Cade fought back a brief moment of jealousy, then realized he wasn't really jealous at all. Gray had finally found what he wanted, the missing piece in his life.

He stole a brief glance at Rocky, unsure why his gaze had drifted that way at all, but he knew, as the song said, that he wanted to find what he'd been looking for as well.

7

*S*imon sat in front of Cormac, his foot tapping out a nervous rhythm on the hardwood floors of Gray's living room. He wanted to hear exactly what was going to happen on his twenty-fifth birthday. The date loomed ahead of him, approaching faster than Simon cared to think about. His anxiety definitely had the better of him. He squeezed the arm of his chair and waited for Cormac to explain everything, to take some of this fear of the unknown away.

Cormac, on the other hand, relaxed in the other overstuffed leather chair with a large mug of coffee in his hand. His perfectly pressed tan slacks covered crossed legs that didn't twitch at all. The collar of his white button-down shirt peeked out from beneath a black-and-purple argyle sweater. Not a single short brown hair was out of place. Simon grumbled under his breath and crossed his legs. He couldn't stop his leg from jiggling at the knee.

If he were honest with himself, part of his annoyance involved the vampire sitting so casually across from him. His irritation bubbled to a boil as his newfound relative acted as if nothing out of the ordinary had occurred over the past few days. Oh no, not a thing wrong in the world. Simon hadn't almost died, had his magic stolen, mated a werewolf, found out Cormac was his great-great-whatever and a vampire on top of that.

Nope, not a thing unusual. Just another day in the life. Except it wasn't, and change and Simon didn't get along well on the best of days. And today wasn't the best of days. In fact, Cormac's decision to opt out of attending the pack meeting the night before exasperated Simon even further. Gray had been surrounded by his numerous pack members, and there Simon had stood, without a single family member or friend by his side. Not one person to celebrate with him, and the only person who could have been there for him had decided instead to return to his home with little explanation.

Leaving Simon alone. Again. Still. And there he sat without a damn care in the world, acting as if it were just another day and they were sipping coffee because they could. A morning chat just to catch up after being away for a few days. Not like Simon's entire world was up in the air with no safety net in sight.

Cormac leaned back in the leather chair and let out a sigh of appreciation as he sipped from his steaming mug. "Your emotions have the better of you today, Simon."

Simon scowled, his temper proving Cormac's point by getting closer to exploding. "Easy for you to say. I don't know what's going to happen, and with everything else that's going on right now, I don't even know how to begin to not let my emotions get the better of me. Not that you've helped take any of that away." The frustration inside him grew stronger with every word. "In fact, you've added more stress to an already overwhelming situation. So forgive me for being human as you sit there drinking your coffee as if there isn't anything wrong in the world. Oh, but wait. Excuse me. There isn't anything wrong in your world, is there? Just mine. And who cares about that?"

Cormac arched a dark brow and set his mug on his knee. "I don't see how I've caused additional stress for you, child."

"Don't call me child," Simon snapped. "I'm almost twenty-five years old."

"And I'm over ten times that."

Simon huffed. Of course he would rub that in. He didn't even look much older than Simon, more like a preppy James Dean. Simon jerked a hunk of his own hair. The sharp burn of pain helped him pull his focus away from his runaway emotions and back to the task at hand. "I want to know what's going to happen on my birthday, and now you're the only person who can tell me."

"You know, you'll be bald before you're thirty if you keep tugging your hair out like that." His lips turned up in the barest of smiles when Simon let out a little snarl of annoyance. "And it's nowhere near the life-altering event you seem to have made it out to be. Your twenty-fifth is a day that should be celebrated. You will grow into your magic and new windows into your mind will open."

Simon threw up his hands. "New windows? Exactly what the hell does that mean?"

Cormac took another drink before answering. "Think of your magic as one of your daffodils. It starts as a simple bulb, planted in the fall and left to take root over the winter months. Then, in the spring, it begins to grow and develop. Little shoots sprout from the ground. This is your apprenticeship. You've grown and created a base, a stem if you will, to support you."

Simon's leg settled from its bouncing, and he thought over Cormac's explanation. "That actually makes sense." It was something he understood, at least. He did have a base to his magic. Not all of Thomas's training had been wasted, and his grandfather had taught him a few basic skills before his death.

Cormac smiled and leaned forward to pat Simon's knee. "Now, you're ready for the blossom. It's the compilation of your training and growth, and you'll be fully formed. As a daffodil."

His soothing tone helped settle Simon's anger. Simon grinned and relaxed back into his chair. "I'm not sure how Gray would feel about me sporting a bright yellow head. But hey, I'll give it a try if that's what it takes."

"I have a feeling you could turn orange with purple polka dots, and your mate wouldn't mind."

Simon looked down at the T-shirt that had caused Gray to snort that morning. A bright orange piñata floated across his chest with the words *I'd Hit That* inscribed beneath it. "Well, he does seem to appreciate my fashion sense."

Cormac glanced at the shirt for a moment, and then his eyes widened as he choked back a laugh. "Does that mean what I think it does?"

"Probably." Simon grinned, unrepentant.

"Only you." Finally a break in Cormac's cool, calm, and collected demeanor. Simon's T-shirt collection amused him, and it seemed it amused his new mate and new vampire grandfather as well.

"Now, back to our discussion. On your birthday, I would like to step in to serve the role of your training master."

Simon nodded but couldn't stop his mind from flashing back to the gruesome image of Cormac's face covered with Thomas's blood. His track record with master mages currently stood at 0-1. His light mood evaporated.

"I'd like that," he said, although his tone showed his lack of confidence in the likelihood of their success. He couldn't even force faked enthusiasm at this point.

"Simon, I know things have been stressful for you, but you need to use the remaining time you have before your birthday to focus on staying centered and balanced. Most apprentices are secure in their power by this point in their training. When Thomas stole your magic, he took more than just the magic itself. He took those years that you would have used to grow accustomed to your power."

"And, big surprise, now I'm not where I need to be." Simon's emotions surged, like a yo-yo spiraling down and then swinging back up with a snap.

"Not necessarily. The spell we'll do together is more of a formality than anything. It opens those areas of your mind that weren't mature enough before now. I'll be with you, though. And I have a year or two of experience at this, you know."

Simon rolled his eyes. "More like a century or two."

"Well, something like that."

Cormac grumbled as he took a drink of his coffee and found it too cool. Simon took it from his hands and went to the kitchen to get him a fresh cup. Cormac never revealed very much about his past, and Simon had never really pushed to ask. He couldn't focus on that, though. He had time to learn more about Cormac.

He looked out at the minimally landscaped backyard at Gray's and thought about what they could plant this coming summer and fall to have the type of yard he loved to maintain. They should probably clear out some of the pines from the woods closest to the house to give the hardwood trees more room. He could put some perennials around the edges of the house to add some color.

If his magic really was like a plant, maybe all it needed was the right set of hands, and maybe a green thumb, to make it everything it could be. He rolled his eyes at the cheesiness of the analogy. He needed to stop thinking of everything in terms of gardening. All the imagery brought to mind was memories of his grandfather. If his grandfather hadn't passed, none of this would be happening.

Simon returned to the living room with a fresh cup of coffee. He handed it over to Cormac and took his seat again. "So we need to talk about training. Exactly what I need to do. And Gray and I would like for you to work with Garon some as well."

He'd mentioned it to Gray the night before as they lay in bed. Gray had sensed that Simon's nerves were strung tight, so he'd just listened when Simon blathered on about this and that. When he'd asked about Cormac training Garon, Gray hadn't even flinched.

Cormac seemed taken aback by Simon's announcement. "Your mate has agreed to this?"

Simon slapped his hands onto the arms of his chair. "No, Cormac. I just said that because I could. I guess this is how my life is going to be now, huh? No one will believe a damn word I say unless Gray says it first and loudest."

Cormac set his coffee down on the side table and moved to kneel in front of Simon's chair. "Chi—pardon me. Simon, where is this anger coming from?" He laid one hand across Simon's where it lay clenched into a fist against the chair.

With a frustrated groan, Simon lowered his head to their hands. "I'm sorry."

"Don't be sorry. You need to get this out. Talk to me."

Simon looked up and gave Cormac a crooked smile. "You can call me child if you really have to."

"It's just a habit. I'll attempt to break it if it makes you uncomfortable. I remember you as a child, you know. I think of you as that young colt of a boy, all legs and wobbling around trying to find his way. But you cannot distract me from our discussion. What is on your mind?"

With everything going back and forth in his mind, Simon thought wobbling was an apt description. "It's okay. I'm just pissed off and can't seem to wrap my mind around all the reasons why. Everything, I guess. That's the way it feels anyway."

"Then let's put them out into the air. Say what's on your mind."

Simon gave his hair another sharp tug, and Cormac reached up to remove the tangled strands from Simon's hand. "Say it."

"Fine. You shouldn't have killed Thomas." Simon's anger heated his face to a deep red. "I shouldn't have mated Gray. My magic shouldn't be this fucked-up." His voice rose and became shriller, but he couldn't stop the rush of words now that he'd started. "My life shouldn't be so damn dysfunctional. I just want things to go back to the way they were before all this started." Simon screamed the last into Cormac's upturned face. The hot burn of tears formed behind his eyes, and he reached to tug at his hair angrily.

Cormac caught his hand in midair and clasped it between his own. "Good. Now let's break it down further. Why shouldn't I have killed Thomas?"

Simon stopped and tried to rationalize why he felt that way. He squeezed Cormac's hand in his and tried to anchor himself. "Because I wanted to know why. What did I do to deserve that? Why me? What did he plan to do with my magic?"

"And those are very valid questions. I want to know the answers as well."

"You had to kill him, though." Gore-covered teeth, blood dripping over Cormac's chin when he lifted his face from Thomas's neck. Simon shivered. "Part of me knows that, I guess. The other part wishes you could have just conked him over the head so we could have questioned him."

Cormac ran his thumb soothingly over the back of Simon's hand. "I could have done that. You're right. But do you understand why I didn't?"

"No."

"Because he hurt you, and in that moment, seeing you lying there on the ground bleeding, I lost control. I'd just found you, and I almost lost you. I must confess that I don't feel bad about it, Simon. Especially now that I know he'd stolen your magic. Only his death brought it back to you, so if nothing else, a bit of good came out of his death."

Simon squeezed Cormac's hand, then tightened his grip further. His voice dropped to a whisper. "I'm glad I got my magic back. But I didn't want him to die."

"I know that, child. You're so bighearted, and no, don't shake your head like it's a bad thing. You were made to love, Simon. Built for it, I think. It doesn't make you weak. It gives you strength."

"But I trusted him. I thought the entire time he was helping me. And I felt so bad that I kept failing him at every turn. He made me feel that way. He made me feel so terrible and inept. And I took it. And the next time, I took it again, and again. For over four years, I did nothing while he stole my magic from me. Ignorant."

Cormac lifted his hands to Simon's face and cradled his cheeks against his palms. "You are not ignorant. You are not inept. Thomas failed you, not the other way around. Would you say these things to Garon? When the demon siphoned Garon's energy, did you blame the boy? Call him ignorant and inept for not being able to defend himself?"

"Of course not. It wasn't his fault."

"Exactly. And it wasn't yours. If you want to be angry with me over anything, this is what you should choose. When you lost your grandfather, I should have stepped in then. You went without support for so long that when Thomas did come along, claiming to help, you didn't know any better. I should have prepared you more, stepped up when your grandfather could not. That is my failure."

With a heavy sigh, Simon leaned his head into Cormac's palm. "I guess in a way, you're right. I wish you had helped me then. When Grandfather died, I went into this shell. I wanted to become a mage to honor his memory. You were doing what my grandfather asked of you, honoring his memory just as I did. He shouldn't have asked you to stay away from me, even if he thought it would protect me. I refuse to be angry with you for that. If he'd known what was to come, he wouldn't have asked you to stay away from me. But he didn't, and neither did you."

"It's difficult not to be angry with him. I wanted to tell you my story sooner, explain who I was to you. When we lost him, I wanted to tell you that you weren't the last mage of your line. You're right, though. If either of us had known that my being both vampire and mage would protect you instead of putting you in danger, we would have made other choices. Hindsight."

Simon straightened his head and covered Cormac's hands with his own. "We lost time, Grandfather. We can't make that up. But I hope from now on, you'll be here for my important moments."

Cormac smiled, although it didn't quite reach his eyes. He stepped back and settled into his chair, then lifted his coffee to his lips. He grimaced at the coolness of it again but drank it anyway. "I'll do my best. And you know, if we went back and changed things, you would not have your mate. If anything good has come of this, it is the fact that you found Gray. This is where you are meant to be, Simon. I feel it with everything I am. I hope you'll begin to accept it soon as well."

8

---

*A*fter following Rocky around for a few days working on the compound's security system, Cade found himself with a classic case of blue balls. He adjusted his stance a little to ease the painful ache in his crotch. Rocky worked like an automaton. His focus remained on getting the equipment up and running as quickly as he could, regardless of whatever, or whoever, hovered around him. He certainly didn't seem to notice that Cade's dick stayed pressed against the fly of his jeans the entire time they worked.

Cade followed his instincts and Gray's order to keep an eye on Rocky. But something else about the visiting wolf drew Cade to him. Sure, part of it was Rocky's looks. Cade liked the long, lean, and lanky thing he had going for him. And his smell. God, he smelled fantastic. After a day spent doing manual labor, they both dripped with sweat. Rocky's musk drew him in, the heat of man and hard work intoxicating. Every time Cade got a whiff of Rocky, he wanted to lick him clean. And damned if his cock didn't twitch and try to push its way out of its denim confinement at the idea.

Cade hadn't quite figured out the other part of his attraction. He considered himself a pretty sexual creature. He liked sex and a lot of it. Women, men, shifters, humans: it didn't really matter to him. Gray and Liam had teased him when they were younger saying he was bi-curious, but Cade never thought of his sexuality that way. He'd tried to explain his idea to them once, but the moment they'd heard Cade say "souls," they'd run for cover. That was how Cade thought of it, though. He didn't see the outside package so much as he saw what was on the inside.

He'd learned at a young age not to judge on appearance alone. As one of the only pack members of color, he'd often believed everyone looked at him differently. No one came out and said anything, but as a kid, Cade had always known his skin didn't look the same as the other cubs'. Add to that the fact that he was at least a head taller than most of the pack by the time he'd made it through puberty, and Cade had always stood out based on his appearance.

So he tried to look at what was on the inside. It was one reason Cade didn't really have a problem with Gray mating Simon. He might be a mage, but Cade could see the beauty in his spirit. Something else he couldn't really explain to his two best friends. They'd fall over laughing and make some crude joke about him being a romantic cheese dick or something.

Then again, maybe Gray wouldn't make fun of him, since his mate had him seeing things differently too. After Gray's formal announce-ment to the pack about his mating, some of the members weren't as happy as Cade thought they should be. He understood their hesita-tion, even if he didn't like it very much. Gray wanted to alpha his way through, to force Simon's acceptance past the few dissenters. He didn't have to. Cade figured Simon would prove himself to the doubters, just by being himself. It would take time, but Cade had no real worries that once they learned *who* Simon really was, they wouldn't care *what* he was.

For Cade, his eyes had opened to Simon's true nature the moment he'd saved the alpha-heir for the second time. Watching Garon struck down by the spell that demon had put on him? Man, it had nearly ripped Cade's heart out of his chest. He'd never felt so helpless. Nothing he could do would save his alpha's son, the boy Cade thought of as a nephew and as close to his own child as Cade might ever see.

Simon had done what they couldn't and had almost killed himself in the process. That type of sacrifice? The willingness to give up your own life to protect the ones you loved? Yeah, Cade understood that. He'd do the same thing for Gray, Garon, or hell, any other member of his pack.

So yeah, Rocky's looks weren't the only thing that drew Cade to him. There was something different about him, something Cade hadn't quite put a name to yet. But he would. He just needed a little more time.

Cade went into the kitchen and grabbed a steak from the fridge. What he really needed was to not think for a while, and the best way to do that was with a nice thick steak, a cold beer, and one of his guilty-pleasure DVDs. And if that guilty pleasure happened to involve watching a certain male character get naked once in a while, well, that only made things better. And if said character happened to slightly resemble a certain visiting wolf wandering frequently through his thoughts, well, that only made things better too.

With his broiled steak and a baked potato plated up and an ice-cold beverage in hand, Cade set himself up in front of the television to vegetate for a while. Hot TV guy was getting busy with one of his cast mates, making out sans shirt, with his rippling abs and treasure trail barely peeking over the hem of his low-waisted shorts. Cade had a good fantasy going with him and Rocky and a hot tub when there was a knock on the door. Cade groaned and dropped his head back on the cushion. He paused the DVD with a grumble and answered the door.

Rocky stood on the other side, dressed in his usual workout clothes. His sleeveless white T-shirt clung to his pecs, the material thin enough that his dusky nipples showed through as little dark shadows. Cade kept his eyes above the waist, even though he wanted to do a full-body scan.

"Hey, man. What's up?" He wondered if Rocky had a treasure trail.

"Not much. I'm feeling the need to let the wolf out a bit and was wondering if you were interested in going for a run. Thought, if you wanted, you could show me some of the shifting stuff we talked about. If you weren't busy or anything."

Cade sighed. He wasn't going to get to see hot guys making out on TV. So much for the distraction of television getting his mind off Rocky. Maybe he'd be able to come up with a new fantasy, this one involving getting a good workout with a certain redhead that he couldn't get out of his thoughts.

"Yeah, we can do that. Just give me a couple minutes." He stepped back inside and carried his half-consumed dinner into the kitchen.

Cade powered off the television and went out onto the porch. He pulled his T-shirt over his head and tried to find the right mind-set for training. A horny teacher wasn't the best teacher. If Rocky wanted to learn to shift more easily, Cade needed to concentrate on helping him.

Rocky's gaze locked onto Cade's bare chest before he jerked his gaze to the side. Cade noticed the look but pretended like he didn't. Rocky removed his own shirt and laid it over the porch railing. The night air held a bit of a chill, not enough to be really cold, but enough to help Cade keep his mind off hot sweaty sex and focused on the task at hand.

"First thing you need to think about is that shifting isn't really a process. You can't think about it like one of your security systems or some computer thing. It's not a step one, step two, step three kind of thing. Most wolves think of the change as a procedure, but it's really more of an instant thing. When you can get your head around the idea that you can shift everything at the same time, you can do it faster. Get me?"

"Yeah. I think." Rocky closed his eyes for a minute, and Cade could feel the wolf in him stirring. "Okay, let's do it."

Of course, Cade's mind went to a totally different place at those words. He should probably make a trip into town for a little stress relief soon. He watched Rocky strip off his shorts, and he did the same. There really wasn't much point in hiding his state of arousal, and Rocky definitely took notice of the huge dick standing straight out in front of Cade.

"Sorry, man. It happens."

Rocky nodded and looked away.

Cade shook his head. It would be nice to at least get a little reaction out of the other guy, especially one who had kept him so tied up in knots for a week. He huffed out a breath and focused.

"So just think of it as one solid movement. You're a man, then you're a wolf. There is no middle ground. Like this." Cade took a couple of running steps and leapt, transforming into his wolf as he flew through the air.

He watched Rocky over his shoulder and saw him shudder a minute before he completed his shift. Rocky jumped off the porch and landed a couple feet from Cade. Cade stepped closer and bumped their heads together, letting his wolf get the scent of Rocky. It wasn't really necessary, but Cade wanted to get a good strong whiff of him, so he did. Rocky let him rub his face and snout over his neck.

Rocky's smell intrigued Cade. There was something unusual hiding in the midst of the scent of his wolf, but Cade couldn't define it. He took off running with a little yip. Rocky followed behind him, and they ran through the night. They dodged low-hanging branches and fallen limbs as they raced through the dark woods surrounding the cabins.

Cade outpaced Rocky quickly and slowed up to let the smaller wolf catch him. They ran side by side for a while until they came to a small clearing tucked into the woods. Cade stopped and shifted back to his human form.

"We'll have some privacy out here. This is where Gray, Liam, and I used to practice when we were cubs."

Rocky shifted back and knelt on the ground, panting slightly from the run. "Man, you're fast."

Cade shrugged and climbed up onto a nearby rock. "I've got long legs. Okay, so here's what I want you to do. You've gotta trust your wolf and make the leap, so to speak." Cade leapt again, transforming in midair. When he landed, he shifted back. "Like that."

"How the hell do you do that? Doesn't it wear you out?"

"Not really. It did at first, but it takes more energy to focus on each step. If you can just let the shift happen, the change isn't as hard."

Rocky climbed up on the rock and looked over at Cade. "You sure about this?"

"Yep. Go for it."

Rocky squatted down, then pushed off with a huge jump through the air. He wasn't quite transformed when he started to land, so Cade caught him to keep him from getting hurt as he hit the ground. He rubbed his hand over Rocky's head, scratching a bit behind his ears. "Better. You were close. Try again."

Rocky shifted back to human, and they ended up kneeling in the grass facing each other. Rocky's pale face showed clearly in the moonlight, and Cade licked his lips, wanting to taste the trickle of sweat that ran down Rocky's temple and over his cheek.

He followed the little droplet of sweat as it ran down Rocky's face and dripped off his jaw to the ground. He glanced up and realized Rocky was watching him. Cade's skin heated in embarrassment.

"Again," he said to break the silence.

Rocky got to his feet and returned to the rock. He looked over his shoulder at Cade before he raised his left leg to climb up. His hips spread, and his back slightly arched. Cade caught a glimpse of his balls dangling low, then he jerked his gaze back up to Rocky's face. And again found him watching.

From the top of the rock, Rocky turned, and Cade realized he'd grown hard as well. Their eyes met, and Rocky jumped, beginning his transformation in midair. He landed smoothly, all four paws meeting the ground. The wolf lumbered over to Cade and sniffed his throat. Cade shivered as Rocky's cool black nose trailed down his chest and over his abdomen. Rocky sniffed lower, and Cade trembled in response.

He reached his hand up and ran his fingers over the rough fur at Rocky's neck. It rippled under his touch as Rocky transformed back into a man. They both panted for breath as Rocky knelt in front of him again.

The sharp snap of a branch breaking sounded off to the side. Cade threw his arm in front of Rocky for protection. Rocky had the same idea, and their arms collided with a smack. The intensity of the moment faded, and Cade rubbed the sore spot on his arm. The woods returned to their previous noises. Cade couldn't pick up any sounds that weren't supposed to be there. He kept his senses alert.

"Want to try shifting again?"

Rocky shook his head. "I think I've done enough for now. I need to do some work on the monitoring system so I can get it transferred over to Gray's house."

"You work too much."

Rocky ignored him and stretched his arms up over his head.

Cade gasped out a breath. His gaze traced a path from Rocky's arched neck to his taut stomach and firm dick. The temptation to drop to his knees and swallow Rocky down was nearly impossible to resist. He had to do something to get rid of the ache in his balls, and sucking Rocky off would go a long way toward getting some relief of his own. His dick was still hard. Now wasn't the time, but damned if he didn't need a distraction. "Race ya?"

He didn't wait for a reply but began his shift and tore through the woods back toward the cabins. He heard Rocky yelling behind him and then more padded footsteps running over the crackling under-brush. Cade ran faster. When he reached the steps of his front porch, he shifted and had his clothes back on before Rocky ran up behind him. "Slowpoke."

Rocky shifted and glared at him. "You cheated." He laughed through his glare, though, and grabbed his pants. "Man, I really hope I can get as fast as you are one day. I've got to give that much to Gray. If nothing else, he knows how to keep his wolves strong." He took a couple deep breaths to get his breathing back under control.

Their run and the shifts had taken their toll, but Rocky was still aroused. As was Cade. Rocky's still thickened cock disappeared beneath his shorts. Damn, Cade wanted a taste of it. The scent of his arousal grew stronger, and Rocky's breath sped back up. The spark of awareness between them built again.

Cade stepped closer and reached out to touch Rocky, but Rocky backed away.

"Okay, I'm going to get to work. You want to work with me tomorrow on some of the martial arts moves?"

"Yeah, sure." The words came out of Cade's mouth, even though his body screamed its disapproval.

"Night."

"Good night."

Rocky wandered off toward his cabin. Cade stood there staring after him for a long moment. Rocky's words didn't sit right with him. What did he mean by "if nothing else"? Gray was nothing if not a strong alpha. As far as Cade was concerned, Gray was a great every-thing—alpha, father, friend. Gray was the kind of man, and the kind of wolf, Cade strove to be.

If nothing else. He couldn't get the statement out of his head, even when he went back to watching his DVD. His mind drifted back to Rocky standing outside, his skin pale in the night. Cade's dick filled at the thought. He hadn't imagined Rocky's responses to him, the way his breath sped up and his cock thickened. Rocky had been into Cade, so why had he run away?

The actors on-screen got hot and heavy. Cade jerked off in time to their thrusts. He closed his eyes and imagined Rocky lying over him and came moaning Rocky's name through clenched teeth.

9

*S*imon and Garon slowly circled the pond tucked away near the back of the pack's compound. The low chirrup of young frogs filled the otherwise quiet afternoon. It seemed like months ago that Gray, Simon, Garon, and some of the other pack members had played here before having a cookout at Gray's. Actually, it had only been a week or so ago, and Simon couldn't believe how much everything had changed in such a short period of time.

Garon focused on the ground, trying to find one last plant for the challenge Simon had given him. They would have to head back to the house soon, as it was almost sunset, but Garon was determined to find one more plant he could identify.

Simon and Garon spent time together nearly every day working on different plants and their uses. When Simon told him that they could find some of the plants just by walking around the property, Garon didn't want to wait. He'd grabbed Simon's hand and pulled him out the door.

Simon spotted a sassafras seedling not far from them and wandered toward it. Garon followed him without really noticing where Simon led. He spotted the distinctive leaf after a moment and hurried over to it.

"Hey, Simon, is this—"

Before Garon could finish, he jerked his head up and turned toward the woods behind them. Simon's gaze followed immediately. Although he couldn't see anything, he could feel a tingle of unfamiliar magic. It drew closer to them at a fast pace.

Simon jerked Garon behind him and called out to Gray through their mind-link. Gray, I need you down at the pond. I feel magic approaching, and I don't know what it is.

He could feel Garon connecting with his father as well.

I'm on my way, Gray responded. He left their connection open, and Simon could hear Gray calling other pack members to aid them. With Gray on the way, Simon focused his attention on the approaching magic and prepared to defend Garon. He drew his power to the surface, sparks of green energy dancing from the ends of his fingers.

His primary focus became building a shield around Garon, and he began forming a barrier similar to the one the demon had built to cage the cubs not long ago. This one wouldn't keep Garon trapped, but it would help prevent any wild magic from coming too close to the boy.

Garon poked his head around Simon's back. His smaller body trembled and pressed closer. "Simon, it's not something bad. It's hurt."

Simon was getting the same vibe, but an injured creature could be even more dangerous than a healthy one in certain situations. But as Simon completed the spell around Garon and opened his magic to reach out to the approaching being, a piercing pain shot through him. It was heartbreak and despair, hunger and thirst, fear and anxiety.

After a moment, a small creature emerged from the woods. A mountain lion cub whose light tan coat blended with dark spots to keep it camouflaged in the woods. It caught sight of Simon and Garon and hissed, its tiny fangs bared toward them. When they didn't move, it curved around behind a rock and lapped thirstily at the pond water.

"Simon," Garon whispered, "it's a shifter."

"I know," Simon said softly. He could feel the cub's magic better now and recognized it as the same type of body magic the wolves possessed. "Let your dad know we're okay, would you?"

Garon nodded against Simon's back, and Simon felt him communicating with Gray through their mind-link. Simon took a step forward. The cub backed away and hissed again. He concentrated with his magic and tried to feel for any magical damage to the cub. He didn't find any.

"It's okay, sweetie. You're safe here. We're shifters too. You'll be okay."

Simon could see the disbelief in the cub's amber eyes. "Can you shift? I need to make sure you aren't hurt, okay? I can get you help."

The cub looked over Simon's shoulder and hissed again. It began backing away from them in fright. Gray emerged from the woods behind Simon with Cade, Rocky, and a couple other pack members at his heels. Simon glanced over his shoulder to let his mate know they were really okay.

"This is our pack alpha. His name is Gray. I'm his mate, Simon. And this is Garon, the alpha-heir. We won't hurt you, I promise."

Gray spoke to Simon through their link. *Is he hurt?*

I'm not sure. He's in pain, but it feels more emotional than physical. He's hungry, I can tell you that much.

Aunt Maggie is making dinner. Do you think we can get him up to the house?

I think so. Can you and Garon back away for a minute and let me try?

Garon walked carefully over to his dad, keeping his movements slow. Simon stepped forward just a few steps and watched the cub's ears flatten out and the fur on its neck rise.

"Shh. It's okay. Come on now. Shift for me."

The cub shook his head, and Simon knew he understood.

"Can I come a little closer? I just want to make sure you're okay." He went forward a couple more steps, then dropped to one knee. "Come on. You can do it."

The cub seemed to give up his fight and slunk slowly toward Simon. Simon held out his hand with his fingers curled under. The cub sniffed him, then jumped up into his arms.

Simon saw Gray start forward out of the corner of his eyes and shook his head. Gray stopped, and Simon turned back to the bundle of shivering fur in his arms. "Shh. It's okay. I've got you. You're safe now." He felt a shimmer of magic and was suddenly holding a shaking little boy in his arms. His tawny blond hair was caked with dirt, and his body seemed too thin.

"I... I'm really hungry," he stammered out with a little cry.

"Okay, sweetheart. Let me take you to my house, and we'll get you something to eat, okay? Can you tell me your name?"

He nodded and sniffed. "Riley."

"Hi, Riley. Don't you worry. We'll help you."

Riley started crying and threw his arms around Simon's neck. Tears formed in Simon's eyes as he stood up and lifted Riley with him. He carried Riley over to Gray and Garon, who petted him gently.

Riley turned to look at Gray and whimpered. "Y-you're an alpha?"

"Yes, I am. I'm Alpha of the High Moon Pack. Where are you from?"

"Th-the Blue Ridge Pack."

Gray thought for a minute and nodded. "In North Carolina. Just over the state line. You're quite a way from home."

"Momma told me to run and to not stop when the bad man came." His tiny body continued to shake. Simon couldn't imagine what would cause a mother to send a boy who couldn't be more than six out on his own. It must have been something, or someone, truly horrible. A mother's instincts were rarely wrong.

Simon and Gray locked eyes, and Simon gently ran his hand down Riley's back. "It's okay, now. We'll take care of you and check on your mom."

The four of them made their way back to Gray's house. Cade and Rocky hovered behind them several steps. Garon ran ahead once the house was in sight and came back out with an old pair of his pajamas when they reached the porch.

After getting Riley dressed, Gray waved Cade and Rocky into his office. He sent a message through the mind-link to Liam.

Gray and Simon settled Riley in the kitchen with Aunt Maggie and Garon. She set aside the heavy meal she'd started in favor of soup and sandwiches. Riley slurped up the noodles and made a mess as the chicken broth splattered unnoticed across his face.

"Slow down, buddy." Gray knelt next to Riley and laid a gentle hand over the boy's. "You'll give yourself a bellyache if you eat too fast."

Riley nodded, but both Simon and Gray could see the boy was starving. He must not have eaten for days. Simon didn't know how long it would take for the cub to run from his pack to theirs, but it had to be a while. Had Riley not eaten in all that time?

Gray gestured for Simon to follow him out of the kitchen. They made their way into Gray's office. "What do you think happened?" Simon asked.

Gray shook his head and grabbed his phone off the desk. "I have no idea. I don't like the sounds of that at all. I'm going to call their alpha. I think I have his number around here somewhere."

A quick search of his address book and Gray dialed the number he had for the Blue Ridge Pack alpha. It rang several times before going to voice mail. Simon went around the desk and stood next to Gray. Gray reached out and grabbed his hand, linking their fingers together. "I'll figure it out, Simon."

"I know. I guess I've got worst-case scenarios running through my head. Why would a mother tell her child to run away?"

Gray gave Simon's hand a little tug, and Simon sat down on his lap. "I'm going to send Liam over there with a team. They aren't under our Were Council, but weres tend to stick close together. Actually, I only know of one other mountain lion pack, and they're out West somewhere. I'll have to check into it."

"What's going to happen to him?"

"I don't know, babe. We'll have to take it as it comes. For now, we'll keep him safe here, okay?"

"Yeah." Simon's head jerked up, and he looked toward the kitchen for a moment before climbing off Gray's lap and heading into the other room. Gray followed behind him. They found Riley huddled in a corner with Maggie and Garon standing close to him. Riley saw Simon and ran for him.

"You left," Riley cried against Simon's shoulder.

"Oh, sweetie. I'm sorry. I just went into the other room while you ate. I'm here." Simon glanced over at Gray, unsure what to make of Riley's reaction.

Gray appeared just as puzzled as Simon felt.

"He was doing fine," Maggie whispered, "then he looked up and realized that Simon wasn't here."

Garon huddled next to his dad and seemed about to cry himself. "He was so scared, Dad."

"Well, I'd imagine so. He's in a strange place and all. He'll need some time to get used to us."

Simon carried Riley over to the stool at the counter where he'd been sitting and sat down with Riley still in his arms. "Did you get enough to eat, buddy?"

Riley nodded, and clenched his fingers in Simon's shirt. Simon rubbed his back and leaned his cheek onto Riley's hair.

Maggie watched them for a moment, then winked at Simon. "You know, I made Garon some banana pudding for dessert tonight, if anybody wants some."

Riley looked over at her suspiciously. Garon, on the other hand, ran for the cabinet with the bowls. "Riley, you've got to try this. She makes the most awesome banana pudding ever."

"Okay." Riley sat up a little but didn't release his hold on Simon's shirt. Maggie served them each a heaping spoonful out of the bowl. Riley took a tentative bite before looking over at Garon with a smile. "It's good."

"Told ya! She puts extra cookies in it 'cause that's how I like it."

"I like cookies too."

"And she doesn't put a lot of bananas in it either, 'cause I don't like them when they get slimy."

Simon shared a look with Gray while the boys devoured their dessert. *You think I should stay with him?* Simon asked through their link.

He seems to feel safest with you around. Probably because you aren't a were.

Okay, I'll stick close. Simon felt another pack member approaching and turned toward the front door. *Liam?*

Yeah. I'm going to go talk to him. I'll have him get a few pack members together to head over there now and check things out. Gray pressed a quick kiss to Simon's forehead and ruffled Garon's hair as he left to let Liam into the house.

Riley leaned back against Simon's chest with a huge yawn. "That was really good," he mumbled.

"Why, thank you," Maggie said. "Now, I think someone needs a quick bath and a little nap. What do you think, Simon?"

"Yep, I definitely smell something funny." Simon sniffed at Riley's neck and made a silly face. "Whew! Stinky!"

Garon giggled. "Don't worry, Riley. He says I'm stinky all the time too."

Riley grinned at both of them and yawned again. Simon carried him upstairs to the hall bathroom and started filling the tub with warm water. Riley stood there, blinking sleepily. "Come on, kiddo. Let's get those jammies off and take a bath, okay?"

Riley nodded and stripped off his clothes before climbing into the tub. Simon handed him Garon's watermelon-scented soap and a washcloth so he could get himself cleaned up. Maggie brought in another set of clean pajamas and laid them on the counter. "I'm going to make a few calls and see if I can round up a few changes of clothes for him. I think some of the other boys in the pack will have a few things he can borrow for a couple days."

"Thanks, Maggie. I hadn't even thought of that."

She gave him a quick smile and left the room to make her calls.

"Simon? Can I be done now?"

Simon looked back over at Riley, who seemed barely able to hold his eyes open. "Just one second, little man. Let me wash your hair. It's pretty dirty."

Riley sighed and nodded. "Don't get soap in my eyes."

"I'll try not to." Simon helped Riley lay back in the water and cupped water in his hand to wet his hair. He used a bit of the bodywash to suds up the dirty strands, then repeated the process to rinse it out. "There. That'll do for now. You ready to get out?"

Riley climbed out of the tub, and Simon handed him a towel. He half dried his body and reached for the clothes on the counter. Simon had to chuckle as Riley tried to pull them over his still damp skin, and they stuck a bit on the wet parts.

He gave Riley's hair a brisk rub with the towel and led him into Garon's bedroom. The spare twin bed was covered in the same moon-and-stars patterned comforter as Garon's bed. Simon pulled back the covers and patted the mattress. Riley climbed into the bed. Simon tucked the blankets around him.

"Will you stay with me, Simon?"

"I sure will. Will you be okay for just a minute? I'm going to go get my book. I'll be right back."

"Promise?"

"I promise. Just close your eyes, and I'll be back before you know it."

Simon double-timed it downstairs to the little room at the back of the house he used as his workshop. He grabbed the book on herbology he'd been studying with Garon and pulled another book on were-creatures from the shelf. With a new breed of shifter in his life, Simon would need to add another subject to his ever-growing study list.

The drive to the mountains surrounding Asheville crept on for what felt like hours. Cade sat in the backseat of Liam's SUV, and Rocky sat in the front passenger seat beside Liam. Cade couldn't keep his gaze off the other wolf, even though Liam had smirked at him in the rearview mirror multiple times.

The animated voice of the GPS indicated that they'd reached their destination, and Liam stopped at the end of the driveway. An old metal gate leaned precariously to the side, doing nothing to bar their entry.

Cade shivered. No pack he'd ever heard of would be so lax with their security. His stomach flipped.

"We go in?" Liam's voice dropped the way it did when he prepared for a fight.

"Let's get it over with." Rocky sounded less sure than Cade, and that said something. Cade wanted nothing more than to turn around, go home, have a steak, and pretend none of this had happened.

Liam glanced in the rearview at the other pack members in the vehicle behind them before beginning down the gravel driveway.

Silence. The only sound around them was the crunching of their tires. Cade rolled his window down and focused his senses. Not a single bird tweeting or cricket chirping. Several small houses appeared at the end of the drive.

Set up as a cul-de-sac, each house faced the large circle. No one came out to greet them.

Liam parked and climbed out. "Hello?" he shouted, the words echoing back. "Anyone here?"

"Shit," Cade mumbled. "This can't be good."

A wooden swing set sat abandoned at the edge of the end house. Liam jerked his head in that direction, and they started toward it. Cade clenched his fist as they walked. A hand brushed his back, and he jumped.

"You okay?" Rocky whispered the words, but all the pack members could hear it.

"Fine."

Rocky nodded and scanned the area around them. Still no movement. Liam stepped up onto the porch and rapped on the door. "Hello!" he called again. After a moment of no answer, he tried the door.

"Oh fuck."

Cade shook his head. Liam turned and walked back out to them, and his face had lost all color. "One dead in the living room."

He gulped and let out a breath. "Okay, let's spread out and check the rest. Cade and Rocky, start across the way. Guys, take the woods, but don't go far. Chris, with me."

Liam and Chris entered the house, and the other wolves went

around the back. Cade followed Rocky across the drive to the opposite house. Rocky knocked on the door and opened it.

He called out when he stepped inside. "Hello?"

Cade thought of one of those horror movies where the idiot calls out for the crazy murderer, like they expect the dude to reply. *Shit.* He followed Rocky inside and listened for any sound that would clue him in that they weren't alone. Nothing. Just that eerie silence that surrounded the mountain lion pack's compound.

They made a quick sweep of the kitchen and didn't find anyone. No one in the bedrooms either. Cade went to the back door and pushed it open. It took his mind several seconds to process what he saw.

A group of bodies lay on the ground at the edge of the yard. He couldn't tell how many. They'd already started deteriorating. He ran toward them anyway, hoping for the best. The bodies were shriveled and shrunken. Cade flashed back to the body of the demon that had tried to kill Simon. When it had been drained, this was what it had looked like. Then he saw a smaller figure, and when he recognized it, he ran away from the bodies and threw up.

Rocky followed and draped his arm over Cade's back. "It's okay, man. It'll be okay."

No, Cade thought, *it'll never be the same.* Seeing the drained body of a child would haunt him for the rest of his life.

10

Two hours later, Riley still napped in Garon's room. Simon sat diligently at his side. Gray walked up the steps slowly, not wanting to wake the sleeping boy and not wanting to tell his mate what Liam and the others had discovered.

It hadn't taken long to assemble a team and get them across the mountains. What they found there had horrified Liam so much Gray could hear it in his voice. Simon looked up from his book and smiled when Gray pushed the door open.

Simon's expression quickly faded when he saw the devastated look Gray couldn't keep off his face.

What happened? Simon asked through their mind-link.

Liam just called. Gray stopped, not wanting to continue.

Oh no. Please tell me it's not the worst.

I wish I could. All of them are gone.

Gone?

Dead. All of them.

Simon covered his mouth to hold back a gasp. Gray crossed the room and knelt at Simon's feet. He took his mate's hands in his and held them tight. How could he tell Simon the rest? How could he not?

Simon, that's not all.

Simon squeezed Gray's hands so tightly his knuckles turned white. Gray stared down at their joined hands and cringed at the tension he could see throughout his mate's body.

Please, Gray. Just tell me.

Gray searched Simon's eyes for a long moment. They were drained, just like the demon was when we found it.

Simon lowered his head to Gray's shoulder and crushed Gray's hands with the intensity of his grip.

It's not over, is it?

No. I don't think it is. Liam is on his way back. I told him not to touch anything. I thought we should have Cormac go.

Simon let out a shuddering breath against Gray's shoulder. He raised his head.

Gray hated the pain he could see in Simon's face. *That's good. He'll be able to tell us if...*

I hope so. But I think we should assume the worst here. The likelihood of it being unrelated isn't good, you know? I've never heard of anyone or anything capable of draining another creature's power. To have two so close together like this?

Simon nodded. I know. You're right. God, Gray, what are we going to do? And what about Riley?

We'll keep him with us until I hear from the Council. Several representatives are going to come for the mating celebration, and we'll make a decision then.

All of them, Gray?

Gray knew what Simon was asking. Liam had been very clear that there hadn't been any survivors of the attack. *Yes.*

Even the cubs?

Yeah, sweetheart. Even the cubs.

It wasn't the demon, then. No way did it have that much power, or it wouldn't have been so crazed when it came after me. It couldn't have been strong enough to take out an entire pack, or it could have easily overpowered Liam and me.

Gray hated thinking of the demon attacking Simon. He'd never forget getting that message from Liam through the link. He'd understood Simon's desire to be in his own home and hadn't been able to force him to stay with the pack, as much as he'd wanted to even then. Thank God he'd set up protection for Simon. If Simon had been on his own that day, Gray didn't know if Simon would have survived. Liam had saved Simon and brought him back to the compound, where he'd stayed since.

You're right. I don't think it was the demon either. Gray stood up and pulled Simon with him. He leaned against his mate, needing the reassurance of Simon's presence.

It couldn't have been Thomas.

Gray agreed with that conclusion as well, but he couldn't be sure without more information. *I don't know. We need to talk to Cormac. And we'll probably need to question Riley more.*

Oh God. How are we going to tell him?

A large tear fell from the corner of Simon's eye and made its way down his cheek. Gray brushed it off with his thumb and wished he had an easy answer. So much had changed in their lives over the past few weeks. There were moments when Gray looked at Simon and could see the grief in his eyes, in the way he held himself.

I think he knows. He may not understand it, but he would know that his connection with his alpha was gone. I think that's part of the reason why he's latched on to you. You were the first person he saw who didn't scare him. We'll talk to him together, okay?

Riley began to whimper in his sleep and sat up in bed with a scream. He leapt toward Simon the moment he saw him. Simon held him tight. Gray leaned in as well, his chest a solid wall against Riley's shivering back. "It's okay, little one. We're here. You're safe."

"Simon? I want my momma."

"I know you do, sweetie." Simon laid his cheek against Riley's soft blond hair and looked up at Gray. His green eyes shimmered with tears again. Gray would do anything to take that look away from him.

Aunt Maggie stuck her head into the room and wiped away a tear of her own. "You guys want me to reheat dinner? Neither one of you ate earlier."

Gray had given her the news before he came upstairs. He hadn't told Garon yet, but Gray would do that as soon as they got Riley calmed down. As hard as it would be to break the news to his son, Gray wouldn't keep the truth from him any more than he could have kept it from Simon. Gray sent her a grateful smile over his shoulder. "Thanks, Auntie. Yeah, if you don't mind, I think we both need to eat something."

"No problem. You guys come on down when you're ready."

Gray, Simon, and Riley made their way down to the kitchen after giving Riley a few more minutes to settle down from his nightmare. Maggie had their plates fixed and sitting on the counter, and Garon sat at the table with a box of LEGOs. Riley's eyes brightened a bit at the sight of the little blocks. He went over to ask if he could help Garon build his toy.

With the boys entertained, the adults sat down to eat. Gray devoured his pork chop and snagged a second one from the serving plate before Simon had even gotten his cut up. Gray looked over at his mate, who had his knife poised over the chop, and found Simon staring at him with wide-eyed shock.

"I was hungry."

"Uh-huh. There's this little thing called chewing. You should try it sometime. It aids the digestion, so they say."

A little light had returned to Simon's eyes. Gray wanted to see more of that, to hear Simon laugh a little. Hell, even a smile would do. He stabbed the meat with his fork and lifted the entire piece to his mouth. He ripped off a chunk with a growl and shook his head menacingly. The boys giggled behind them.

Simon glared over his shoulder. "Don't you two take his side. That's disgusting."

Simon couldn't hide his little smile, though, or the twinkle in his eyes. The boys laughed harder and turned to see what Gray would do next. He wiggled his eyebrows at them before waving his half-eaten chop under Simon's nose. "Mmm. Meat. Tasty!"

"Oh, whatever," Simon groused. Then he took a huge bite and attempted a snarl. Gray snorted and turned back to his plate. Simon knocked Gray's elbow with his own, causing the potato Gray had just picked up to plop back onto his plate with a splatter of gravy.

"Oh, that's it. You've done it now." Gray turned back to the boys, who were still avidly watching the show. "Let's get him, guys!"

Simon tried to scramble away, but Gray moved faster and pulled him back against his chest. Garon leapt into the fray, tickling Simon's ribs and causing Simon to shout for mercy. Riley watched them play for a few seconds before he dove in as well. His little fingers tickled Simon's stomach. Simon made sure to laugh and squeal for him too.

After a few more minutes, Simon called a halt to catch his breath. Garon leaned against him, still laughing. Riley climbed up on Simon's lap and grinned at him. "You're really ticklish."

"Yeah, yeah. I'll get you back."

Riley snickered and glanced down at the food that remained on Simon's plate.

"You hungry, sweetie?"

Riley eyed the meat and looked back at Simon.

"Go ahead. I'm full."

As Riley attacked the meal, Gray and Simon looked at each other, the reminder of the ordeal the little boy had been through suddenly back at the forefront of their minds. Simon leaned his cheek against the back of Riley's head for a moment, then leaned over and kissed Gray's cheek.

"Liam's here," Gray said against Simon's ear.

"Okay. You want me to see if I can get the boys settled in upstairs?"

"If you don't mind."

"Sounds like a plan. We'll head on up, and I'll be back as soon as I can."

Gray ran his hand through Simon's hair and pulled him in for a quick kiss. Riley shifted on Simon's lap and looked over his shoulder at the two of them before making a face and turning back to scrape up the last bit of gravy.

"Get used to it, Riley," Garon said. "They do it all the time. They're in love."

Simon's eyes widened. He turned to Gray with a look of panic on his face that Gray hadn't seen before.

"Yes," Gray confirmed, "we are. And if you two don't watch it, we'll be kissing all over you next."

"Eww!" Riley hopped down from Simon's lap as he yelled along with Garon. The two of them ran upstairs with a thunder of footsteps.

Gray snagged Simon's hand when he went to follow. "I know it's soon, but I do love you."

Simon took a deep breath and let it out slowly, then looked up and met Gray's eyes. "I think I love you too. It's so... I don't know."

"I think *soon* is the word you're looking for."

"Maybe so. I like this feeling, Gray. I like being here with you, as much as it terrifies me."

"It'll get easier, and I'll be here, right by your side."

"That's the best part."

"Simon!" Garon bellowed.

Simon laughed and went toward the stairs. He turned back and smiled at Gray once more before hurrying to see what Their Royal Highnesses required.

Gray sat back in his chair and ran his hand over his beard. Damn. He really did love Simon. It had kind of snuck up on him, but that fluttery feeling in his chest had to mean love. He had never felt this way about anyone, he knew that much.

Liam, come on into the kitchen, he said through his mind-link before rubbing a hand down the front of his body. The thought of Simon gave him this little high, a burst of happiness and contentment. Damn. It must be love.

Liam took one look at him smiling goofily and rolled his eyes. "You do realize you're setting yourself up for lots of jokes, right?"

"Whatever," Gray scoffed. "I remember a time or two that I can get you back with. Oh, maybe... Ryan? Wasn't he the hot bear?"

"Shut up."

"Uh-huh. I thought so."

Liam sat down on Simon's abandoned stool. His expression sobered. "That was the most horrible thing I've ever seen."

Gray laid his hand on Liam's shoulder and squeezed. "I'm sorry."

"Don't be. We had to know. I'd rather it was me than someone else."

"How did Cade handle it?"

"Not well. He found the first of the kids. Damn. He's shut down. Rocky went with him to his cabin. Said he'd stay close for a while so I could update you."

As tough as Cade appeared on the outside, Gray and Liam both knew how much something like that would have affected him, especially after the kidnapping of their cubs mere weeks before.

Gray didn't think Cade would be the same after all of this. Hell, he wasn't sure Liam would be the same. His beta's eyes were haunted in a way they hadn't been when he'd left. Another layer of resentment formed against whoever was doing all this.

"Have you called Cormac?"

Gray forced his thoughts aside. "Not yet. I told Simon, but then we had to take care of Riley for a while. We just finished eating."

"Got enough to share?"

"Of course." Gray got up and cleared his and Simon's plates away. He pulled a clean dish out of the cabinet and set it in front of Liam.

When Liam's plate was filled and he began eating, Gray slipped out of the room and went to his office to call Cormac. The vampire answered the phone a bit brusquely.

"Yes?"

"Good evening, Cormac."

"Oh, hello, Gray. My apologies. I'm in the midst of research and loathe being interrupted by inane telemarketers."

Gray laughed and breathed a sigh of relief that Cormac wasn't angry with them for some unknown reason. "Well, I'm sorry to bother you as well, but we've had a new development that I'm afraid we need your help with."

"Is Simon okay?" Gray heard the slight tremble in Cormac's voice, and remembered the loss he'd seen on Cormac's face when Simon chose to become Gray's mate instead of letting Cormac turn him into a vampire. As Cormac's only living relative, Simon meant more to him than Gray could begin to understand.

"Simon's fine. This afternoon at the lake, we discovered a mountain lion cub. I tried to contact his pack and didn't receive an answer, so I sent Liam with a team to investigate. The entire pack had been killed and drained, similar to the demon."

"Good Lord. Everyone?"

"All of them. Except Riley, whose mother told him to run."

"What can I do?"

"I thought you could go over there and see the scene yourself. Maybe there's something in the magic that you can detect that we can't."

"Yes, I can do that. Gray, be vigilant. This does not bode well."

"Understood. I'll have Liam take you over there. It's about an hour's drive."

"Should I come to the compound?"

"How about I have Liam pick you up? When you've done what you need to do over there, he can bring you back here. We can determine what to do next."

"Agreed. How is Simon handling the news?" Cormac's tone softened, his concern for Simon's well-being apparent.

"Not well. And Riley has latched on to him for some reason. I can't figure out if it's helping keep Simon's mind off things or if it's keeping his mind on the situation. You know how he can be."

"Yes. He'll have to find a way to process the details in his own time. Caring for Riley will help."

"I hope so. I hate seeing him so upset over this, especially with everything else he still has on his mind."

"Just be there for him, Gray. This mating of yours is new and fragile. Cherish it, and him, and you'll be fine."

"I will. I'll see you when you get back. Take care of yourself."

"Thank you, Gray. We'll get to the bottom of this."

. . .

To call the mood in Gray's office the next morning grim would be a huge understatement. Rocky sat along one wall and watched the others in the room. The alpha sat behind his desk. Lines of tension cut across Gray's face, and his coffee mug sat untouched next to him.

Gray's expression matched the others in the room. Rocky's gaze flitted over to Cade, who sat slumped in one of the chairs in front of Gray's desk. Although Rocky had followed Cade to his cabin the night before, the other wolf hadn't allowed him inside. He'd put up a wall so high that Rocky hadn't been able to break it down.

This morning, the results showed on his face. Deep circles under Cade's eyes made him appear haggard. His lips were pinched, and he clenched his hand into a fist on his lap. Hell, even his clothes reflected his mood—black cargo pants and a black tank top.

Gray called the meeting to discuss the newest round of events to affect the pack. When Cormac returned, late, from his visit to the murdered pack, Gray asked them all to be at his house first thing in the morning.

Cormac's cultured voice drifted over to him, and Rocky forced his attention to the matter at hand. "I've never seen such powerful magic before. The strength it must have taken to subdue an entire pack, to force them to watch as they were systematically destroyed, is more than I can imagine." His words lodged in his throat, and the vampire stopped speaking.

Liam looked as shell-shocked as Cormac. "Gray, there is nothing left there. We brought back what records we could find, as well as a couple computers from the alpha's residence. We photographed everything before we began the burial process. The rest of the team is working on that now."

Rocky shivered. The pack beta had obviously helped with part of the burial process. His jeans and blue T-shirt were streaked with dirt, and his eyes were glazed. Rocky could imagine what they'd had to do but tried to force the images out of his mind.

"How many?" Simon asked.

"Twelve. Three cubs."

Damn, Rocky thought. They'd only seen one cub the day before, and Rocky had figured the cub got caught up by accident. He'd never heard of something that would take out everything, including the cubs. From what he'd seen the night of the attack on Simon, there was a lot he hadn't heard of, and none of it was good, from the sound of things.

"Is there evidence any others escaped?" Gray didn't sound like he held out much hope, and Rocky imagined he was right. Something powerful enough to take out an alpha wouldn't want to leave any loose ends behind.

"No," Cormac answered. "I think Riley is the only one who escaped, and I'm not sure how his mother knew to have him run."

"She must have told him to go before the killing started," Liam added. "I don't see how he could have escaped otherwise."

Rocky wondered the same thing. It seemed fishy to him. And dangerous.

The topic of discussion turned to the little mountain lion shifter that they didn't know what to do with. Rocky knew what his vote would be, even if it wouldn't be a popular one. He'd get that kid away from the pack so fast the boy wouldn't know what hit him. Especially considering that Cormac had seconded Liam's conclusion as to what had happened to the mountain lion pack.

Something had drained them of their magic. Problem was, no one knew what that something was. Could have been another demon like the one that had taken the High Moon Pack's cubs, or maybe another mage like the one who'd attacked Simon. All Rocky knew was that the little lion boy might as well have a target on his chest, and whatever had taken out the rest of his pack would be after the boy next. This pack already had enough troubles without borrowing more. Completing the security system became more urgent as the minutes passed.

Rocky leaned back and let the discussion flow around him. He wasn't really surprised that Gray, Liam, Cormac, and Simon disagreed with his unvoiced opinion to get rid of the kid. Cade hadn't spoken up, but Rocky didn't doubt he'd agree with them too. Just another example of how different things were in this pack.

His alpha would never allow a stray to stay with their pack, child or not. There were too many variables and threats down that path, and the pack's safety should be the alpha's number-one concern. But Gray wasn't as hard-core as his alpha, a fact that Rocky feared would come back to haunt him sooner rather than later.

Simon perched on the arm of Gray's chair, his mate's arm tucked around his waist to hold him in place. Rocky tried not to stare, but his gaze kept darting over to them. They puzzled Rocky. They had met just a few short weeks ago, but the connection between them grew tighter with each passing day. The bond crackled. Even Rocky's less-than-stellar nose could smell the arousal in the air whenever the two of them crossed paths.

He'd heard some rumbles from other pack members that Simon had doubts about the mating too. *Yeah*, Rocky thought. *I'd be having major doubts.* Their mating would never be allowed in his pack. It held no purpose, at least according to his alpha's rules. True mates should be able to procreate and make more of their kind. Of course, Rocky himself didn't plan on having children, so he supposed any mating he did would be considered useless as well. No way would he bring a cub into the world to be an omega like him.

This pack didn't seem to care at all. Rocky wondered if it was because Gray already had an heir. That must be it. Otherwise, they couldn't accept the mating. Then again, the High Moon Pack seemed to do a lot of things differently. Nothing about them made any sense. Maybe if they were like his pack, the cubs would never have been taken. Gray seemed tough enough to earn the title of alpha, but sometimes Rocky wondered if he had what it took.

Rocky forced his mind away from his musings and refocused on the task at hand. The sooner he got Gray's security system up and running, the faster he could get out of here and on to his next job. If Malone would let him, that is.

"Rocky?"

Gray's voice caused Rocky to jump. Everyone in the room was staring at him. He turned his attention to the alpha. "Yes, sir?"

"Do you think you can get into one of the computers and see what you can find?"

"I can try." He shrugged. "I'm not a hacker, by any means, but I can see if it'll boot to a CD. If it will, I can probably get access to the contents of the hard drive."

"Good," Gray answered before he turned to the others. He scowled after a second and turned back to Rocky. "Does that mean someone can do that to my computers too?"

Rocky nodded. "If you have a determined hacker who knows what they're doing, not much will keep them out. I'd worry more about stopping them from getting into the compound than protecting what's locked on your computer. Once they've made it this far, I'm not sure what the point is."

"Good point. We'll talk more about that later." Gray's attention turned back to the others in the room. "Liam, I want you to tackle the written records you recovered. Cormac, we need any information you can provide on the culprit. We're out of our league here in terms of magic, and you're our only resource. I'll report our findings to the Council and go from there."

"But we're keeping Riley?" Simon turned on the arm of the chair, and Gray nodded. Rocky tried not to shake his head at the riskiness of the decision.

"Yes, we're keeping Riley. At least until we hear from the Were Council."

"I'll need to question the boy." Cormac drew their attention.

Simon started to protest, then snapped his mouth shut and nodded.

Rocky twisted in his seat and propped his ankle up on his knee. Someone needed to question the boy, if for nothing more than to determine how big a security risk he would be.

"You'll... be careful with him?" Simon might not want the boy traumatized, but Rocky figured they didn't have a lot of choice. At least they were seeing reason on that front. Cormac hadn't answered

Simon's question, and Rocky turned to see the vampire glaring at Simon. Another moment passed before he answered.

"Of course, Simon. Did you really need to ask?" Cormac waited until Simon shook his head to acknowledge his question. Then he continued. "But if there is any information he can provide on the so-called 'bad man,' we could use it. And I'd like to step up your training, Simon. The threat has not passed. We must be prepared for another attack on both you and the pack."

"Agreed." Gray turned to Simon and ran his free hand down Simon's leg. "I want to know you can defend yourself as much as possible."

"You don't have to baby me, Gray. I can take care of myself." Simon brushed Gray's hand away and stood. "But yes, Cormac, I'd like to intensify my training. Because I need to, not because I've been told to."

An uncomfortable silence filled the room. Liam cleared his throat as he stood and gave a slight bow of his head to Gray. "I'm going to get started on the paperwork. I'll keep you informed." Cade also nodded to Gray before following Liam out of the office.

The intense look shared between the alpha and his mate had Rocky following them. "I'm going to go grab something to eat. Alpha, I need to test the system and will need access to the computer for at least an hour, possibly two."

"Just come back when you're finished eating. I want this system ready to go as soon as possible."

Rocky headed back to his cabin with his thoughts in a jumble. There was so much confusion in his mind that he wanted to keep working and force his thoughts away from the circles of information running through his brain. Maybe a run in his wolf form would calm him down. An image of Cade popped into his mind, running through the night and shifting with ease. A brief moment of peace came over him. Maybe he could talk to Cade about some of his concerns.

The other wolf seemed to keep cool in a crisis, but today wasn't the best day. As one of the alpha's closest friends, Gray would likely listen to Cade over him. He started down the path toward his cabin, shoving aside his plan to stop at Cade's first.

The intensity of their attraction should be enough to keep him away. Whatever was between them, he couldn't let his emotions get in the way of the job he'd been given by his alpha. Rocky shook his head and decided to try to work through his problems on his own. It was probably better that way. The less confusion he had to deal with right now, the better. And dealing with Cade left him with more questions than answers.

11

*C*ormac didn't waste any time putting Simon to work with a new training regimen. He taught Simon not only how to keep his magic centered but also to unfurl the power at different speeds: slowly when he needed to coax and quickly when he needed to defend.

They stood together in the yard behind Gray's home. Simon still had trouble thinking of the house as his as well. Cormac tapped Simon's shoulder to regain his attention. Looking at the vampire reminded Simon of his doubts in having Cormac question Riley. He'd been really good with the little boy, even though they hadn't been able to get any new information from Riley. All he knew was that his mommy had told him to run from the bad man and to not stop.

Cormac's brow arched at Simon's continued lack of concentration. Simon gave him a sheepish grin. "Sorry. I have a lot on my mind."

"Focus, Simon. Now, center yourself. Ready?"

Simon nodded.

"Begin." Simon closed his eyes and drew his power close. He sensed the moment Cormac drew his own power close, and he prepared to defend himself. His hand came up without conscious thought, and his magic deflected the spell Cormac flung at him.

"Very good. Again."

It amazed Simon how different the training process felt with Cormac. Without the so-called "training bond" Thomas had insisted they needed, Simon's magic answered his slightest call. Now, of course, Simon understood that Thomas had used the bond to steal his power, but at the time it had shaken his confidence in his abilities. He only had a few more days to get his mind wrapped around his recovered powers before the "grand opening," as he'd begun to think of his approaching birthday.

Cormac's second attack slipped through. Simon's distraction cost him a sharp sting to his arm where the spell hit. He rubbed his arm for a moment and tried to concentrate on the task at hand. The miss shook his confidence, and Cormac's next attack dealt him another bite of pain.

His lack of certainty showed through many times, and as Cormac stomped his foot and yelled in frustration, Simon began to understand what Cormac meant when he said Thomas had stolen more than just his magic.

"I'm sorry, Grandfather." The endearment came more naturally now. Strange as it was, Simon felt the same deep affection for Cormac as he had his own grandfather. The vampire's expression usually softened when Simon used it. This time, it didn't.

"Simon, I understand this is difficult for you, but you have to learn how to defend yourself against th—" Cormac stopped and ran his hand over his short dark hair.

"Against who?"

"Against the weres, Simon. Against the wolves you hold so close to your heart."

Simon stepped back, the hot rush of betrayal starting in his stomach and rolling through his entire body.

"Simon, just listen. I know you love this pack, but there are other packs, other creatures, who are not so welcoming. Didn't you wonder why we kept ourselves apart for so many years?"

"My pack won't turn on me, Grandfather. They won't."

"I believe you. The problem is that *other* packs may. You're different, Simon. So different from the others. Some won't like that. You *must* be able to protect yourself."

"I *want* to be able to protect myself." Simon sat down next to the big oak tree in the backyard and leaned against its trunk. Cormac came and knelt beside him.

"Our power only works against weres when they are in their human forms. We cannot control the mind of an animal."

"But—"

"But nothing, Simon. We can't. I know the wolves have their own abilities. I know that you can communicate with them, but you cannot control them. That trick you pulled with the humans? When you distracted them and saved the cubs? Mind magic isn't effective on a wolf."

"It worked on the demon, though."

"That's right, it did. I know it's confusing, but magic interacts differently with other types of magic. Think of it as a garden. No. You know what, you know this. I shouldn't have to keep sugarcoating it for you."

Simon stopped and thought. Gray's magic did feel different. So had the demon's. He'd never tried to stop a wolf, but he had stopped the demon, even if it was only for a short time. "Okay. I understand."

"Good. Now, to stop a wolf, we cannot do any of our mind tricks that work on humans, or even those with soul magic, like myself. What are the strengths of the wolf?"

"They're strong and fast, and they have heightened senses."

"Yes. Now, you can't cloak yourself, because that hides you from the eyes, but not from the nose or ears. What else?"

"I would need to be silent." Simon looked up, realization dawning. "No, I don't have to be silent. Silence stands out as much as loud noises. I have to blend in with the other sounds around me."

"Good."

"So that spell you were showing me, heightening awareness of my surroundings and amplifying the energy, that was to protect me from the wolves?"

"Yes. Aggrandizing is a complicated process, and the spell is not one hundred percent foolproof. It's a giant step above the basic cloaking and camouflaging you've already mastered. As you said, if you can trick a wolf's smell and hearing, you can get away."

"And sometimes getting away is more important than staying to fight."

Cormac nodded. "We all must defend ourselves to the best of our abilities. There will be times when you'll have to stay and fight. We'll work on those situations as well. But if you can, you run. Understood?"

Simon sighed. "Gray would say the same thing."

"Of course he would. He wants you safe."

"And I want to keep them safe. I know you guys don't think I can defend myself, and maybe that's true right now, but I want to learn. I want you to teach me. With everything going on, I need to know that my family can count on me. And my family includes you, Grandfather."

Cormac didn't seem to know what to say. He stared at Simon for a long moment, then reached out and pulled Simon into a hug. "I will do anything to keep you safe. And I'm honored you would do the same for me."

Simon heard the slight hitch in his voice and pulled back to look at Cormac's slightly flushed face. "Let's get to work. I've got a family to protect." He grinned and sent a wave of magic through his hands and into Cormac.

Cormac threw his head back and gasped. "You are so strong, Simon. Just the touch of your magic is enough to refill my stores."

Simon shrugged. "I'm not really trying to give you any or anything. I just wanted to show you that I could call my power fast, like we've practiced."

"Hmm," Cormac murmured. "We'll need to consider this. If it wasn't intentional, this could be a gift of yours. But that is for another day. I want you to practice the aggrandizing spell."

Simon pushed a gust of breath from his lungs and began to draw his power around him as he'd been taught. As he inhaled, he swept his right arm down his body to form the cloaking spell, and his left swirled around in a circle to agitate the particles in the air surrounding him.

Once they were in disarray, he focused on specific elements. He enhanced the scent of the earth beneath his feet and the damp leaves in the underbrush. Next, he turned to the sounds of nature, strengthening the brush of leaves as they rustled in the wind and the faint sound of critters as they scuttled through the woods.

The process only took a few moments. Simon turned to Cormac, who stared in his direction with awe. "Brilliant, child. You did it. I can sense your presence, but only because of our connection. I cannot see or hear you. We'll have to have one of the wolves tell us if you have covered your scent."

The news thrilled Simon, and he knew just the wolf who could help. He sent out a silent call to his mate. *Gray? Do you have a few minutes to help me with a spell?*

I have the boys with me. Let me see if Rocky would mind keeping an eye on them for a few minutes.

Will Riley be okay?

We'll see. I have him distracted with a computer game at the moment, so I think we'll be okay for a little while. This kid loves to play games just as much as Garon.

A moment passed while Gray spoke with Rocky and the boys, and then his voice was back. Okay, Rocky will stay with them, and Riley said he wanted to stay and keep playing. Where are you?

Simon grinned. *You'll have to find me. Marco...* He turned to Cormac, who continued to stare in Simon's general direction without seeing. "Grandfather, my mate is on his way to find me. Would it be too rude for me to ask you to leave us?"

"Certainly not," Cormac replied. "My presence might give something away and negate the effectiveness of the test. You'll give me the results of the spell?"

"Absolutely. Well,"—Simon smirked— "maybe not *all* of them."

Cormac blushed and seemed to realize from Simon's tone exactly what he had in mind. Simon hadn't seen the vampire move so quickly in the entire time he'd known him, but by the time he heard the back door opening, Cormac was gone.

"Rocky?"

Gray's voice broke Rocky's concentration, and he turned to the alpha.

"Would you mind hanging out here with the boys for a little while? Simon needs my help out back."

Rocky looked up at the alpha in horror. He couldn't stop his reaction. "Um, me?"

"Yeah, you." Gray seemed amused by his reaction. "Garon, you okay working on your project for Cormac a bit longer?"

"Yeah, Dad. I've almost got it done."

"Riley, you want to keep playing your game?"

Riley scowled at the screen for a moment before turning to Gray. "Uh-huh. This is fun."

"Alright, I'll be in the backyard if you need me. Gar, just call me if you need me and Simon to come back inside."

"Okay."

Gray turned back to Rocky.

Rocky finally composed himself enough to answer. "Uh, sure. No problem. You won't be gone long, right?"

Gray laughed as he stood and shifted Riley from his arms back into the chair. "Shouldn't be more than a half hour or so."

"Okay."

Rocky sat stunned in Gray's office as the alpha exited the room and left him alone with Garon and Riley. Garon lay on the floor with an encyclopedia of plants open in front of him. He'd scattered colored pencils around a pad of paper and concentrated on drawing one of the leaves displayed in the book. Riley continued playing the computer game, and the beeps and whistles assured Rocky that he knew what he was doing.

His presence didn't seem to bother them, so Rocky continued

testing the security equipment. They'd worked quietly for some time, with the only noises the clicking of keys on Gray's computer and the occasional commentary from Riley as he played his game. Rocky found a few sensors that needed to be adjusted and made notes as to what he needed to work on over the next couple days.

Rocky looked back and forth at the boys every few minutes, waiting for some sort of meltdown or something that he wouldn't know how to handle. The boys ignored him for the most part and concentrated on their own tasks, so he turned back to his testing and jotted down a few more adjustments.

"Crap. This is stupid!" Riley smacked his little hand down on the desk.

Rocky turned to see what the trouble was.

Garon's voice drifted up from his spot on the floor. "Riley, Dad and Simon don't like for us to use those words."

Rocky felt like maybe he should intervene, so he walked over to the desk and looked at the cartoon characters dancing across the computer screen. "What's the trouble, buddy?"

"I can't figure out this word. Will you help?"

Rocky's mouth dried out in a sudden rush of fear. His pulse pounded in the veins of his forehead, and he took a deep breath. The kid was what, five? Maybe six? Couldn't weigh more than forty pounds. He could do this. "Uh, well, yeah. I can help."

Riley climbed out of the chair. He looked at Rocky expectantly. Rocky took the hint and sat down behind the alpha's desk. Riley climbed up onto his lap and pointed to the screen. "What's this word?"

The characters moved around on the screen, but they waited on Riley to answer the word question at the bottom. Different letters floated around, and Riley needed to pick the one that made the correct word. "Okay. I think they want you to spell what this guy has on his head, right?"

"Yeah."

"And what is that?"

"Oh, a hat," Riley answered.

"So let's find the missing letter."

Riley stared at the screen, his tongue out as he concentrated. After a moment he scowled in frustration. "I can't remember what an *h* looks like. It makes the 'huh' sound."

"Right." Rocky didn't know if he was supposed to give the answers, but he pointed to the lowercase *h* hovering around the characters anyway. "Try that one."

Riley dragged it into place with the mouse. The characters cheered and moved on with the game. As tempted as Rocky was to move Riley back into the chair and go back to his own work, he kind of liked being able to help, so he stayed put.

The mountain lion cub wriggled around after he answered another question correctly. Riley knew his shapes, but still had trouble with his letters. He got the next couple questions right, and after another few minutes, the game let out a series of whistles and horns and flashed "Level Complete" across the screen.

"I did it!" Riley cheered and leaned back against Rocky's chest with a big smile. He tilted his head back to make sure Rocky was watching. Rocky smiled down at him, nearly struck dumb by the bright smile.

"Good job, Riley." Garon poked his head up and smiled over the desk at them. "I told you you could do it."

Riley nodded and yawned, his little jaw cracking with the width of the stretch. He turned his face into Rocky's chest and used his arm as a pillow. Rocky sent a panicked look over to Garon, who shrugged. "He gets tired a lot."

Garon lay back down on the floor, and Rocky gazed at Riley. Garon didn't seem to think it was such a big deal, but Rocky wondered if they should call Gray and Simon. The little guy seemed content as his eyes drifted closed, so Rocky decided to hold off for a bit. Gray had said he wouldn't be gone too long. He could handle this.

Riley squirmed and curled up tighter. Rocky instinctively tightened his hold. Riley snuggled closer and grabbed hold of Rocky's shirt. As Riley's body went lax with sleep, protective instincts Rocky hadn't even known he possessed kicked in. Riley's blond hair shone against Rocky's dark shirt. He brushed a strand out of Riley's face, and Riley scrunched up his nose.

He remembered his earlier thoughts about getting rid of Riley and how he was dangerous to the pack. The little boy in his arms proved how ridiculous that notion was. Rocky still wasn't sure if it was *right* to have another were mixed in with a pack, but suddenly it didn't seem so wrong.

*G*ray stepped out onto the back deck and looked around the yard for Simon and Cormac. He sensed something different in the air, but he couldn't locate his mate. He sniffed, then sneezed. Everything smelled really strong for some reason, like it had just rained and the thick scents of the woods flooded the area.

But it hadn't just rained, and his mate was nowhere to be seen. "Simon?" he called out as he searched the area behind the first line of trees. Cormac and Simon often worked there in the daylight hours to take Cormac's light sensitivity into account. His answer was another *Marco* from Simon through their mind-link.

"What the hell is Marco? Where are you?"

He heard a snicker of laughter off to his right, quickly muffled. *You mean you've never played Marco Polo?*

Not since I was a kid. So you want me to find you, huh?

Yeah. And if you can, you get a prize. Simon's brightly colored T-shirt came hurtling through the air and landed on the deck at Gray's feet.

Gray pulled off his shirt, followed by the rest of his clothes. He had no problem playing this kind of game. With a grin, he shifted and leapt off the deck in the direction of the tossed shirt. All his senses were focused on finding his mate. He let his wolf's senses lead him, but he couldn't track Simon by any of his normal methods. After sneezing a couple more times from the potent scents in the air, he gave in and sent *Polo* out to his mate with a huff.

"Marco," Simon whispered off to his left.

Gray turned in that direction in time to see Simon's jeans come floating out of thin air toward him. Gray caught them in his jaws and growled low in his chest. His mate stood out here somewhere, scantily dressed, and Gray couldn't find him.

You are in so much trouble when I find you. He heard another quick chuckle and changed his direction.

Bring it on, big guy.

He tracked Simon through the yard, dropped Simon's jeans at the edge of the trees, and then followed the trail into the woods behind the house. Nothing. He couldn't catch Simon's scent no matter how hard he tried, and he couldn't hear anything other than the rustling of the leaves.

Gray paused and looked around. He peered up into the trees, where they barely shifted in the light breeze. Yet it sounded like there was a heavy spring wind blowing. Puzzling. He continued tracking, his frustration mounting. He resisted as long as he could before he called *Polo* out in his mind and received another whispered clue from Simon in return.

After several failed attempts, Gray stopped and used his brain instead of his senses. When he grew closer to Simon, the sounds and smells grew thicker. If he drifted too far off the path, the intensity lessened slightly. Armed with his discovery, Gray tried again to locate his mate. When his senses began to be overwhelmed, he decided to play dirty. He looked back the way he'd come and took a few steps in that direction. With a final *Polo*, he waited to hear Simon's voice.

The moment he heard "Marco," he turned and leapt. His aim was slightly off, but he still managed to tackle Simon to the ground. Simon eased the cloaking spell and lay on the ground laughing, half underneath Gray's wolf form.

Gray shifted back and laid his naked body against Simon's. "Tag. You're it," he chuckled.

Simon laughed and reached beneath him. He flung a rock from under his back and settled more comfortably against the ground. "Took you long enough. How'd you find me?"

"I followed my nose."

Simon huffed and frowned. "You weren't supposed to be able to find me that way."

"Ahh, but I'm smart." Gray buried his nose in Simon's neck and rubbed his beard across the sensitive skin around Simon's throat. Simon moaned and arched his neck to give Gray greater access.

Gray nipped his way down to the spot between Simon's neck and shoulder where he'd marked him during their mating. He bit a little harder on that still tender bit of flesh. Simon arched and trembled beneath him.

"You're distracting me," Simon moaned, but his protest held little weight as he wrapped his arms around Gray's broad shoulders and drew him closer.

Gray lifted his head and pressed a quick kiss to Simon's lips. When he drew back, he raised his hand and traced a finger down Simon's cheek and over the slight stubble on his chin. "I didn't like not being able to find you," he murmured as he spread his hand and lifted Simon's head to his.

They kissed again, all lips and soft touches. Gray couldn't seem to keep his hands from roaming over Simon. He threaded his fingers through his mate's hair, then down his neck and over his shoulders. When he reached Simon's waist, he tucked his arm beneath Simon and rolled them onto their sides.

Simon tucked one leg between Gray's and wrapped an arm around him to rub over Gray's back. The motion soothed Gray, and at the moment he needed to be calm. The ramifications of Simon's ability began to sink in as the fun of the game wore off. His mate could hide from him or perhaps be hidden from him. Gray had been through that feeling when Garon and the cubs had been kidnapped. His abilities as alpha were cut off from those he'd vowed to protect. The terror of not being able to communicate with his son hadn't worn off yet. It had rushed through Gray at random moments since Simon had brought the cubs home.

As he lay there under the trees with the dappled glow of sunlight shining through the verdant leaves above their heads, Gray realized how much more he had to lose. His son, his pack, and his mate. Any and all could be taken from him at any moment. He shuddered and buried his face in Simon's neck.

He breathed in deeply, the woodsy, sweet scent of Simon's black-berry sage soap soothing him. Simon continued running his hand down Gray's back. Gray wanted to tell Simon the fears revealed by his racing thoughts, but he couldn't force the words out. What if Simon saw him as weak? He fought to get his control back and raised his head to meet Simon's eyes. Simon gave him a little push and rolled Gray over onto his back. He slid on top of him, and they stared at each other for a long moment.

"You are the strongest man I've ever met," Simon whispered. "I never worry that you won't be able to find me. Even with the strongest spell I've ever done hiding me, you still found me. I know you're holding it together by a thread right now and have been over the past few weeks. But you've kept it together and helped me be strong when I just wanted to curl up and hide from it all."

"I don't—"

"Shh." Simon pressed a gentle kiss to Gray's lips. "I'm getting stronger every day. I want you to lean on me this time. I may not be as powerful as you are, but I am strong enough to stand beside you and take some of this weight off your shoulders. Let me be a true mate to you, a real partner. Let me in. Let me help."

"I—"

"The correct answer is 'Yes, Simon.'" Simon smirked and raised an eyebrow that was eerily familiar to the eyebrow Gray often cocked at him.

Gray chuckled.

Simon lowered his brow and laughed as well. "Too much?"

"A bit," Gray replied. "But not the sentiment. I need to know we can get through this. I need to know *I* can get through this. I don't want to lose you, Simon."

"You won't. We're stronger together. Don't forget that. We're doing everything we can to keep our family safe, and we won't stop."

"No, we won't," Gray repeated. He ran his hand down Simon's spine, tracing the smooth skin and warm muscles. "Our family. I like that."

Simon smiled, his eyes bright. "I still don't know what I think about how fast this has happened. It's a whirlwind. But I think I've found the place I'm meant to be."

Gray ran his fingers through Simon's hair and pulled him down for a kiss. "Yeah. I think you have as well."

When they broke apart, Simon gave Gray a mock frown. "You messed up my plan. I figured if I could strip all the way down before you found me, then I'd argue that I got to top. But…" Simon paused and wiggled his boxer-clad groin against Gray's naked one. "Since you found me before I got naked, I guess you get to fuck my brains out. Again."

Gray slid his hands down and squeezed Simon's ass. "As much as I would love to, there's another flaw in your plan. No lube."

Simon scowled and dropped his head to Gray's chest. "Damn it."

Gray laughed and hugged Simon against him. "Don't ever try to take over the world, okay?"

After smacking Gray's chest, Simon raised himself up and began to rut against him. "Who needs the world? I have everything I need right here. Except lube."

They laughed, and Simon dropped his head down to Gray's. They tangled lips and tongues together in a kiss that brought both their cocks to full hardness by the time they were done. Simon continued to jerk frantically against Gray. When Gray couldn't take the wonderful friction anymore, he grabbed Simon's hips and forced him to stop.

"There are other things we can do, you know. For example, if you spun that delicious ass of yours around here, I could take care of that ache you've got going."

Simon moved so fast Gray had to laugh again. He only stopped when Simon knelt over his face, his cock poking through the slit in his boxers and dangling down toward Gray's lips. Simon didn't waste time looking. He dove right down and devoured Gray's cock, licking and sucking the throbbing length into his mouth.

Gray's balls began to draw up, and he tried to fight back the sensation, to make it last. He'd never wanted someone this much, felt such intense desire, longing, need. He tugged Simon's boxers down and pushed them out of the way before he raised his neck and drew one of Simon's lightly furred balls into his mouth. He laved it thoroughly with his tongue and then switched to the other. Simon groaned, the vibrations shooting straight up Gray's spine.

He released Simon's sac from his mouth and turned his attention to the rock-hard length dangling by his cheek. He rubbed his facial hair over it, and Simon jerked in response. No one had ever gotten off on his beard like his mate did. With a grin, Gray ran his chin over the tip and followed it with a wet swipe of his tongue.

Simon whimpered and thrust against Gray's face, so he opened his mouth and swallowed him deep. Simon pumped his hips frantically, and Gray began to push up into Simon's mouth as well. So close. He could tell Simon was as well, their matching paces building, each thrust getting them closer and closer.

With his focus so strongly on Simon, Gray's release crept up on him. He let out a hiss as his sensitized cock jerked and he shot into Simon's mouth. His entire body trembled as his mate swallowed and continued sucking around him as spurt after spurt exploded from his slit. Gray whimpered and cursed himself for making such a sound, before he grabbed Simon's dick in his fist and began to pump at a furious pace.

When he could think without risking Simon's important parts, he slurped the tip back into his mouth and teased the slit with his tongue. Gray could tell from the fluid leaking from Simon that he was close as well. He sucked and stroked harder and faster. Simon began to hump his face, his hips jerking as he finally stiffened and came in Gray's mouth.

Gray held the offering on his tongue. When Simon finished, he spun him around with a wicked grin. He rolled Simon onto his back, his mate's body lax and moving easily. He dove for Simon's mouth. Simon opened for him, and Gray shared the offering. Simon devoured him, sucking his tongue in farther as their flavors exploded between them.

Simon dropped his head and panted up to the sky. "Holy hell."

Gray plucked a dried leaf from Simon's hair and licked a stray drop of come from his lips. "I second that holy hell with a hot damn."

"Next time, I'll remember the lube."

"Next time, I'll let you fuck me."

Simon gasped and grabbed Gray's head, then pulled him back into another kiss. "Maybe later?"

"We'll see." Gray winked and rolled off Simon. "Depends on how good you are."

"Hmph. I'll show you good."

"I'm counting on it." Gray climbed to his feet and reached down for Simon's hands. When they were both standing on only slightly trembling legs, Gray reached down and helped Simon step into his discarded boxers. The trees had sheltered them from view, but Gray kept himself between Simon and any eyes that might be able to see his mate's body.

"Now we should probably go rescue Rocky. He's been in there with the boys for a long time, and from the panicked look he gave me when I left, he's probably ready to be off kid duty."

They walked hand in hand back to the house and stopped to gather Simon's randomly tossed clothes along the way. Gray dressed when they reached the deck, and they went into the office to check on the boys.

Riley was sound asleep in Rocky's arms. Gray chuckled at the somewhat shell-shocked expression on the other wolf's face. "Everything okay?"

"Yeah," Rocky said with a slight smile. "No problems at all."

Gray rounded the desk and reached to take Riley from him, but Rocky stopped him with a quick gesture. "Um, is it okay if I...?"

"Yeah," Gray answered after a moment's pause. "Let's go lay him down. I'll help you." He didn't know what had taken the worried look from Rocky's face, but he could see something different there now. Maybe a little acceptance.

Rocky stood carefully and shifted Riley in his arms so the cub's head lay against his shoulder. Gray led the way upstairs and helped Rocky lower the boy to his bed.

"You know," Rocky whispered, "the longer I stay here, the more I find myself starting to challenge the way I always thought things should be. I'm not sure if that's good or bad, but it's definitely confusing."

Gray laid a hand across Rocky's shoulders, and they started back down the stairs. "Change is confusing, Rocky. It's strange for me too. But sometimes you have to listen to your heart and not just your head. Trust your instincts."

It was the same advice Gray's father had given to him, and he believed it. Those instincts had led him to Simon, told him he should go against tradition and bring a mage into their pack. He felt the same about keeping Riley safe.

Rocky nodded but stopped when they reached the office door. Simon knelt on the floor with Garon, going over the drawings Garon had worked on in their absence. "I'm trying, Alpha. I found some problems with some of the equipment that I'll work on over the next couple days. Just some adjustments to placement, really. But I'll be out of your hair soon enough."

"Rocky, you can hang out a bit longer if you need to. I don't want the security system delayed for obvious reasons, but after that, if you need a place to stay and regroup, you're welcome here."

Rocky shook his head, and Gray realized just how confused he actually was. "I'll let you know. Now I'll leave you to your family."

When Rocky left, Gray knelt by Garon's side and admired his drawings as his son explained the significance of the plants he was learning to identify.

Change. Something told him they all had a bit more to go through before everything was done changing in their pack and in their world.

13

Cade's truck sputtered and coughed for a minute, not wanting to go into town any more than Cade did. He gave her a little more gas, and she started up again. Cade didn't like the sounds the truck was making and made a mental note to take her to the garage and have her checked out soon.

With a pat to the truck's dash for luck, Cade pulled away from the pumps at the gas station and into an empty parking spot. He opened his soft drink and took a large swallow. He checked to make sure the level was low enough. When he saw that it was, Cade dumped in a bag of peanuts. The soda fizzled and fuzzed. Cade took another gleeful drink. This time the sweet was paired with the salty bite of the peanuts.

"And now, we work." Cade chuckled to himself and took another swallow before backing out of the parking spot and heading to Allison's house. As he crunched on the peanuts, he planned how to deal with his client and her blatant attempts to get him into bed. He really wasn't in the mood to fend off more of her advances, and her "broken dryer" was the latest in a string of ploys to upgrade him from handyman to sex toy.

By the time Cade pulled into her driveway, he'd gotten his "work face" on and was ready to deal with her come-ons. He grabbed his tool belt and meandered his way up the sidewalk. After knocking on the door, Cade stepped back and listened. "Shit, I'm not ready!" He heard her exclaim. He had to chuckle at her antics, even if she didn't think he could hear her. Wolf hearing had its benefits.

"Just a minute," she called out, this time loud enough that human ears would pick up the words.

If Cade had his druthers, she would take more than a minute. She wasn't the first customer to come on to him, and normally it wasn't that big of a deal. A few years ago, he'd even taken a fella up on his offer of a blow job. Man, he'd really known what he was doing too. Cade had picked up a few tricks that day.

His problem with Allison was that she didn't seem to take his hints that he wasn't interested. With his mind reeling from everything going on with the pack and his hormones perking up at every stray thought of Rocky, Cade really didn't want to deal with her.

A moment later, the door opened and Allison stood there, slightly out of breath and not wearing a whole heck of a lot. Her pink tank top was pulled dangerously low, exposing the mounds on her chest in an enticing display. And yeah, Cade thought they were nice to look at, and another time, maybe he would have been tempted. But not today.

"Hey, Cade." She smiled and showed off her perfect white teeth and glossy pink lips.

"So your dryer's not working?" Cade figured it was best to get right to the point.

She pouted a bit and stuck out her hip to show off her short shorts. "Nope. The darned old thing just won't dry. I knew you could help."

He fought the urge to roll his eyes at the ploy. "Sure. Mind if I come in?"

"Oh, no, I don't mind. Come on back to the laundry room."

She led the way through her living room toward the back of the house. Everything was pink and floral and smelled a lot like some cheap drugstore perfume. The scent overwhelmed Cade's nose. He covered it with his hand to hold back a sneeze.

When they reached the laundry room, Allison opened the dryer door and bent over in front of him. She looked over her shoulder and made sure Cade noticed her ass, then turned back to grab a handful of damp undies from the machine. "See?" she whispered, dropping a tiny pair of lace unmentionables into his hand. "They just won't dry."

Cade nodded and placed the undergarment on top of the dryer. "Let me have a look."

He pulled the machine out from the wall, and immediately spotted the problem. The venting tube wasn't connected to the wall outlet. He tugged the dryer out farther and stepped behind it to reattach the vent before pushing the machine back against the wall.

Allison practically stomped her foot in frustration when Cade tossed her underwear back in and turned the dryer on. He turned to her with a grim smile. "Well, let's just let them run for a minute, and I'll make sure things are working okay."

She seemed to take his words as an invitation because she sidled up to him and ran her hot pink fingernails down his chest. "I just knew you could fix it. What would I do without you?"

Good grief, the woman acted like he'd invented the damn thing. When her fingers got to the top edge of his jeans, Cade grabbed her hand and gave it a gentle squeeze. "It's no problem, Allison. I don't mind fixing things for you, but that's all I want, okay?"

Allison stepped back and slipped her hand from his grip. "You really aren't interested at all, are you?" She seemed puzzled and hurt, and Cade wasn't sure what to do. Handling a crying woman wasn't covered in trade school.

"I'm sorry. I guess, well, I've met someone I am interested in, and I don't want to mess that up." Cade tried to hide just how stunned he was by his statement. He hadn't even realized it until that moment. He wasn't interested in anyone else. He wanted to know more about Rocky and to figure out what was going on between them. What used to be his standard excuse, the thanks-but-no-thanks line that got him out of uncomfortable situations like this, had suddenly turned into the truth.

He leaned back against the dryer, a little shocked by the realization.

She nodded and leaned against the wall across from him. "You're a good guy, you know?"

Cade shook his head, still trying to process his thoughts.

"You are, Cade. I want to find a good one."

"You will." He forced his mind back to her. "You're a good gal."

She sent a saucy grin his way. "Got any single friends?"

"I'll see." He chuckled and ran his hand over his head. It trembled a little. Nerves? Excitement? He wasn't sure. "Now let me check the dryer."

"No need." She blushed and looked up at him from under her lashes. "I pulled the vent off just so I could get you out here. The dryer's fine."

Cade laughed and turned to leave. "I'll see you around, Allison. Like the next time something is *actually* broken?"

She shrugged and blushed a little, but he could tell she wasn't really all that shaken up. Cade headed back through the house and out her front door. By the time he got to his truck, he was jogging. He really wanted to find Rocky. Maybe he could help do something else with the security stuff today. Or maybe they could do some training.

Cade backed out of Allison's driveway and sped toward the pack compound. His thoughts roamed the entire time, and before he knew it, the gates were in front of him. Cade couldn't even remember most of the drive. When the guard entered the code to open the gate, Cade pulled up beside him. "Hey, Chris. Any idea where Rocky is?"

Chris jerked his thumb over his shoulder. "A couple of the motion sensors weren't lining up properly. He's over on the west side of the property trying to realign them."

"Alright. I'll go give him a hand. Thanks, man. Everything going okay?"

"All clear here."

"Good. Have a good one."

After driving his truck as far down the western path as he could, Cade parked and sniffed the air to get a sense of where Rocky was. He caught a trace of Rocky's scent and took off at a fast walk.

"Rocky? You out here, man?" Cade's stomach flip-flopped a little with excitement. He couldn't see for all the trees and shadows created by the midafternoon sun. With everything blooming, even the scents were overwhelming.

"Cade? That you?"

"Yep. Came to give you a hand." Cade turned a bit farther west and started jogging in the direction of Rocky's voice. A thick layer of pine needles and decomposing leaves from the fall crunched under his feet. It didn't take another minute before he found Rocky leaning out over a tree branch, adjusting one of the monitors.

Cade's heart skipped a beat. The limb bent beneath Rocky's weight. Rocky's body trembled as he tried to keep his balance. "What the hell are you doing?"

Rocky stared down at Cade and scowled. "What does it look like?" He rolled his eyes and stretched out a little farther along the branch.

"Be careful!" Cade yelped, and the sensor tumbled from Rocky's grasp. Cade caught the equipment before it hit the ground. "You shouldn't be doing that by yourself."

Rocky glared down at him. "Oh for fuck's sake, Cade. I do this all the time, okay? What is your problem?"

Cade stared up at him for a moment, then looked down at the device in his hands. He couldn't really explain his issue. How could he? He didn't really understand it himself. *Oh yeah, Rocky. I've just realized I'd really like to get to know you better, see what happens from there. And, you know, seeing you up there and in danger, makes me feel all funny and protective-like.* Fuck. Rocky would either laugh his ass off or try to kick Cade's. "Just come down, would you?"

With another exaggerated eye roll, Rocky slid his legs over the branch and dropped to the ground. Cade stared at him for a long moment before he realized Rocky held out his hand for the motion detector. "Oh. Here."

"Are you okay?" Rocky looked puzzled. Cade had no idea what his own expression revealed. Probably nothing he wanted.

"Yeah. Yeah, I'm fine. Just a weird day."

Rocky shook his head, then went still. He sniffed the air, and his eyes darkened. He leaned in closer and sniffed again. A low growl came out of him. He turned around and dropped his head.

"What's wrong?"

Rocky's body tensed and coiled in on itself. Ready to shift or strike.

"You smell like a woman."

Cade sniffed his shirt and realized he smelled like the cheap perfume from Allison's house. "Fuck. Yeah. One of my customers. Man, her house reeks."

Rocky glanced over his shoulder, and Cade shrugged.

"Seriously reeks. I swear, I thought I was going to sneeze the entire time I was there. Some sort of roses or something." He stepped up to Rocky's back and ran his hands down Rocky's arms.

Rocky leaned back against him, then straightened and went to climb the tree again.

"Let me help?"

"I can do it." Rocky glared, his hands gripping the bark so tightly his fingers turned white with the strain.

"I know. But I can help." Cade kept his voice pitched low—soothing, not threatening.

Rocky leaned his forehead against the trunk of the tree. Cade watched him take a couple deep breaths. "What do you want from me, Cade?"

"Right now? I just want to help."

Rocky tucked the sensor into his pocket and scrambled up the tree. When he balanced on the branch again, he looked down at Cade. Their gazes locked on each other. "Help works for me." He broke their eye contact and took a focused breath.

Cade kept one eye on Rocky as he stretched out again and arranged the sensor. There was something there, something he was missing, but he couldn't figure it out. He thought about the strange reactions Rocky had to him, the way he'd acted when they fought, and then again when they'd trained.

Rocky tilted his head as he stared at the angle of the sensor. Cade had to fight back his reaction. *Shit.* That was it. The way Rocky tilted his head sometimes without thinking about it, the way he submitted as a wolf, how small his animal form was. *Fuck*. Rocky was an omega.

He must have made a noise or something, because Rocky glanced down at him and frowned. "Sorry, just thinking. Everything okay?" Cade hoped his voice didn't reveal anything, and when Rocky turned his attention back to his adjustments, he thought he was okay.

Their pack had never had an omega, but Cade knew they were around. They were another one of those things no one talked about. Sort of like the mages and vampires and the rest. They existed, but that was as far as the information went. Most packs shunned them, Cade had heard that much. But Cade remembered Gray's dad telling them about omegas once when they were younger.

It was during their training, one of those summers when he'd pushed Gray, Liam, and Cade extra hard. He'd made sure they knew that just because a man's wolf wasn't as powerful as another's, that didn't make him weaker. It just made him different.

Cade knew all about being different. But he'd always had his strength as a wolf and his sheer size in his human form on his side.

He wondered if that's why Rocky acted like such a tough guy most of the time. It must be. In another pack, being an omega would be something to be ashamed of. Cade hoped Rocky had figured out he didn't have to worry with them.

Rocky swung down from the tree and landed nimbly at Cade's feet. "Done."

"Great." Cade stepped forward and wiped a bead of sweat from Rocky's brow. Rocky leaned into the touch for a moment before he pulled away and jerked his head to the side.

"Got another one left to fix. You coming?"

"Sure." Cade let Rocky lead the way, his thoughts even more scrambled than they'd been before. What the hell was he supposed to do now?

14

Simon could feel Garon's excitement from across the yard. With Gray's permission, Cormac was ready to begin training Garon in the new powers he continued to develop. Although having multiple types of magic was extremely rare, it did happen. Cormac himself was an example. Having been a mage before the attack that turned him into a vampire, Cormac could still perform some mage-specific spells.

Cormac had explained to Simon that as he'd matured as a vampire, his ability to do other types of magic strengthened as well. Simon wanted to have a more in-depth discussion with Cormac about combined powers like he and Garon had. Simon had a bit of mixed-magic too now that he was mated to Gray, but it didn't compare to the strength he could feel in the pair he watched across the grass.

The sun dipped behind the trees and left the yard in dim enough light that the vampire felt comfortable being outside. Cormac wouldn't turn into a flaming ball of ash if the sun hit him directly, but he did feel more comfortable in the shade. He also grew stronger in the evening hours.

Riley played with Garon's soccer ball near where Simon sat in the grass. Simon had offered to play with him, but Riley wanted to practice hitting the ball with his head like he'd seen Gray do earlier. He threw the ball in the air and whacked it with his head. The ball rolled a few feet away. Riley rubbed his forehead as he chased after the ball and began the process over again.

Simon turned his attention back to Cormac and Garon. They carried a folding table out into the yard. Simon waited to see what Garon's reaction would be to the day's lesson. Garon watched every move Cormac made and copied him to some extent. He'd seen Garon do the same thing with his father. Today, Garon had even dressed like Cormac normally did. He'd worn a shirt with a collar and his nicest pair of jeans.

Gray hadn't said anything to Garon about his choice of attire when he'd noticed the similarity earlier that morning, but he'd asked Simon through their mind-link if he noticed it as well. They'd shared a smile at Garon's show of support for the vampire.

Cormac set his bag of supplies on the table and turned to Garon. "Today, we are going to talk about Cromniomancy, an early form of Divination."

"Chrome. Neo. Mancy?" Garon's jumbled attempt at the word had Simon grinning again, but Cormac didn't seem fazed. He was an excellent teacher, patient and supportive. Not like Simon's training the past few years had been. He was thankful Garon had someone they could trust to teach him.

"Precisely. Now, are you aware of the term Divination?"

Garon shook his head.

"Divination is a way to answer questions, to tell the future, if you will."

"That sounds cool."

"It can be, yes. And Divination used to be a widely studied craft for the mages. Although most forms aren't as accepted today as they were in the past, I want you to be aware of our beginnings." It didn't escape Simon's notice that Cormac still thought of himself as a mage first.

Cormac opened the bag and pulled out a knife, cutting board, and a bag of onions. "Cromniomancy uses onions to tell the future."

"Onions?" Garon turned up his nose and scowled. "That's silly. Onions can't tell the future."

"Yes, onions. Are we going to continue, or are you not interested in learning?"

"I'm interested, but I don't like onions. They stink and make my eyes water. Dad or Aunt Maggie always cuts up the onions."

"You don't have to like them to learn from them, young one. Now, let's take an onion and slice it in half and begin."

Simon watched as the two continued their discussion. Bittersweet memories of his grandfather teaching him the same lesson rolled through Simon's mind. He hadn't understood the significance at the time, but now he could see that learning about plants and their unique properties had always been a priority of his early teachings.

Divination by onion might not be a current method, but by breaking down the plant, studying different areas and layers, Garon would learn to see things as the sum of their parts, instead of just as the whole. He would need that ability the older he got. It was an important skill for controlling the mind magic of the mages.

The soccer ball dropped in Simon's lap, pulling his attention away from the pair at the table. Riley crouched down in front of Simon and pointed to the red mark on his forehead. "I don't like hitting the ball with my head. It hurts."

"Yeah, I suppose it would." Simon rubbed the spot gently. "You want to kick the ball around with me now?"

"No. I want to shift and make my head quit hurting. Can I?"

Simon hesitated for a moment before responding. "Well, I don't mind, but you have to stay right here with me. Can you do that?"

"Yep." Riley stripped off his clothes and changed into his cat form before Simon could say anything else. The speed of the shift astonished him. Riley, even as a cub, could shift as quickly as he'd seen Gray or the other adult wolves shift.

In just a few days, Riley had gone from a scrawny, dirty animal to a gorgeous mountain lion cub with tawny gold fur. Simon saw the difference in Riley's shifted form and sighed in relief. He pounced on Simon playfully and rolled onto his back on Simon's lap. Simon rubbed his exposed belly, and Riley purred as he swatted at Simon's chest with his front paws. When Simon's hand drifted up to scratch at Riley's chest, Riley trapped his hand and nipped at it.

"Hey now, watch the teeth."

Riley huffed at him and scooted his head under Simon's hand.

"Oh, you want me to pet your head, is that it?"

Riley's answer was a rumbling purr. Simon complied with a laugh and ran his fingers over Riley's head and ears. Riley closed his eyes and rolled onto his side. He curled up into a ball on Simon's legs and settled comfortably as Simon continued to pet him.

With every moment Simon spent with Riley, his connection with the boy grew deeper. He already loved him, and although there would probably come a day when Riley had to leave, Simon couldn't help but hope that somehow they could work it out for him to stay with them and become an official part of their family.

Garon came over and squatted next to them. "Can I pet you, Riley?"

Riley stretched out a paw, and Garon ran his fingers over it. "You're really pretty. Simon, can I shift too?"

"Um, well, it's not the full moon, Garon."

"I know. I can do it, though."

Simon looked up at Cormac, who shrugged and left the decision up to Simon. "Okay, but you have to stay with me too. Deal?"

"Sure." Garon stripped and shifted in a fluid movement. His wolf form was the same steely gray as his father's. He appeared nearly full-grown. Still, he tried to climb onto Simon's lap with Riley. He only managed to get his top half across Simon's body and laid his head next to Riley's for a little sniff. The boys rubbed their heads together for a second before they settled and let Simon pet them both.

Gray stepped out onto the back porch. Simon could tell he was surprised to see his son in his wolf form. Although he didn't comment, the look he gave Simon let him know they were in for another discussion later. He crossed the yard to them and kissed Simon's head, then knelt down and petted the boys. "You guys want to play a bit?"

They both perked up and looked eagerly at Gray.

"I'll take that as a yes. Simon, that okay?"

"Of course. I told them they had to stay with me, but if they're with you, that's okay too."

Gray nodded, and Simon could tell he understood Simon was explaining it to Riley and not him.

"Yep. Garon, we're not going to go for a full run, okay? Let's stay close to the house. Riley, will you stay with me?"

Riley jumped off Simon's lap and put his paws on Gray's chest.

"Okay, let me shift, and we'll play for a bit before dinner."

It never ceased to thrill Simon when his mate shifted into his wolf form. As a man, Gray exuded power, but as a wolf he simply *was* power. From the way he moved to the way he looked at Simon with his animal eyes, Simon felt stronger just by being near Gray's wolf.

Their eyes locked on each other's as Gray transformed. One minute, his mate's blue eyes stared at him, and the next the blue eyes were in the face of the wolf. Gray didn't move at first, simply kept their gazes locked on each other. *You're beautiful,* Simon whispered through their link.

Not half as much as you.

The moment didn't last, though, as the cubs both pounced. Gray began chasing them around the yard. He'd nip at one, and then nudge the other off balance before beginning the chase all over again. Cormac knelt for a moment at his side and ran his hand over Simon's shoulder. "You have a beautiful family."

"As do you, Grandfather. They are yours as well."

Cormac's lips curved up in an almost smile, and he turned to watch them play for a moment. "I'm going to go get some work done now. We'll meet again in the morning for your training?"

"I'd like that." Cormac disappeared into the shadows. Simon felt his longing even as they parted. He'd gone from being alone for a few short years, to having a fully formed family when he'd mated Gray, but he still remembered the deep sense of loneliness he'd felt after his grandfather had died and he'd been left on his own.

Cormac had been on his own for so much longer. Seeing the joy in his mate as he played in the yard filled Simon with joy and hope, and he couldn't ever remember feeling either emotion as distinctly as he did now.

He lost track of time as he watched them, but soon his stomach reminded him it was past dinnertime by growling loudly. "Okay, boys, time to eat."

All three of them turned to look at him, and in unspoken agreement, they all tackled Simon to the ground. He lay on his back and laughed as they all licked at his face.

"Okay, okay! Uncle!" Simon tried to sit up but fell back again when they all shifted back and grinned at him. "You guys are awful. Licking a man while he's down is just not fair." He wiped his face in an exaggerated motion and pretended to shake the drool off his hand.

Garon giggled and tickled Simon's ribs. Simon pushed him away with a pretend growl, and they all laughed again. After all his boys got dressed, Gray pulled Simon to his feet and linked their hands together. "Shepherd's pie for dinner?"

"Yep. Aunt Maggie has it ready and said all we had to do was warm it up."

"Man, I love that woman."

Simon laughed and squeezed Gray's fingers. "I bet. She takes good care of us."

"Do you want to get the boys cleaned up, or do you want to warm up dinner?"

"Since you're just as dirty as they are, why don't you guys get washed up? I'll get everything ready."

"Sounds like a plan. Boys, to the bathroom. Simon says we're filthy." Gray prodded them both until they reached the stairs.

Simon listened to them chatting as he warmed up their meal and got the dishes down to set the table. They were back within a few minutes and lined up to hold their now-clean hands out in front of Simon.

"Nope, not clean enough!" Simon declared after glaring at their fingers. Garon pulled his hands up to check, and Simon tweaked his nose. "Gotcha!" Riley giggled and tried to grab Simon's nose in return, but he couldn't quite reach.

"Okay, boys set the table, and we'll get the hot stuff." Gray handed Garon the plates and Riley the forks and napkins. Simon watched them all working and couldn't believe how at home he felt. Until he had this family, he hadn't known that it was what he'd been missing all along. He tried not to worry about Riley's future, but the thoughts were never far from his mind.

After dinner, Gray volunteered to clean up while Simon got the boys ready for bed. By the time he got them changed and washed up, Gray was by his side to tuck them in. Riley looked a little worried, and Simon reassured him that they would be steps away if he needed them.

Gray and Simon decided to turn in as well. Simon needed some time to reconnect with Gray without his thoughts straying to the kids, the pack, the Council, or any of the other problems that had plagued him throughout the day. Gray stripped down to his boxers, and Simon pulled on his Superman pajama pants, much to Gray's amusement.

When they climbed beneath the blankets, they met in the middle of the bed. Simon ran his fingers through Gray's chest hair and let the motion soothe him. His nerves began to settle, and Gray ran a hand up and down Simon's back. "You feeling better?"

"Yeah. It was a good day."

"I know you're worried about Riley, baby, but we just have to wait and see."

"I know. I just can't believe how fast I fell for him. It feels like he's mine now. Is that weird?"

"I don't think so. It's one of the things I love about you. You care so much. Damn, that's cheesy, isn't it?" Gray laughed and rolled over so they faced each other.

Simon rested his forehead against Gray's and smiled. "You know, until I met you guys, I didn't know that I cared like this. I'd been alone for so long."

"And now look at you. You're surrounded by members of the pack all the time."

"It's nice."

"Yeah. If you ever need some space… God, I don't even want to offer that."

"Don't worry. I'll ask."

Before Gray could answer, the sound of little feet in the hallway had them both turning their attention to the door. "Dad?" Garon whispered.

"Come in."

Garon opened the door and peeked his head inside. "Riley's scared. Can we stay in here?" He pushed the door open farther to reveal Riley. The cub had tears streaking down his face.

"Yeah. Just for tonight, though, okay?"

Riley nodded and wiped tears from his cheeks. He climbed onto the bed. Simon and Gray parted to let the boys climb in between them. Once they were settled, Gray stretched his arm out toward Simon, and Simon reached out and joined their fingers together.

ade sat on an old chair he'd dragged out to his front porch, his bare feet propped up on the porch rails. He held a cold beer in his hand and took long drinks of it intermittently. The foam fuzzed in his mouth as the tart brew slid down his throat. The distraction wasn't enough to calm his racing thoughts.

Since he'd figured out Rocky's secret, his mind continued to roll through scenarios. Mainly, he wanted to know why Rocky kept his status so closely guarded. What did it mean? There had to be a reason.

Cade hadn't found very much information in the pack history book about omegas. Nothing that would explain Rocky's reticence to tell them the truth. Then again, Gray probably wouldn't have agreed to let Rocky go on the mission with them to save Simon if he'd known. If nothing else, Rocky was a proud man. A strong man. If circumstances between them had been different, Cade doubted he would have figured out that Rocky was an omega.

The old white tank top Cade wore had pilled after many washings, and Cade picked at the little balls absentmindedly. He wanted to ask questions, to maybe go talk to Gray about it, but his alpha had so many things on his mind right now, Cade didn't want to add to the list. He had to do something, though. He just couldn't figure out what.

With a quiet sigh, Cade took another swig of beer, and it lodged in his throat. He'd never kept secrets from Gray before, and part of him demanded that he go tell Gray everything. But he didn't really know what the ramifications of that confession would bring, and something in him told him to keep quiet for a little while longer. Rocky wasn't hurting anyone by being here, and his secret really didn't make a difference. Well, as far as Cade knew it didn't. He couldn't be sure unless he asked, and if he asked, it might cause more trouble.

Circles. All he could do was think in circles. He took another gulp of beer and tried to find something else to occupy his thoughts. He wiggled his bare toes and realized he should probably trim his toenails. He hated doing it. Something about the clicking sound of the clippers sent shivers down his spine. Feet were definitely not his thing. He'd seen a porn once where the guy sucked on the other guy's toes and moaned and groaned. Cade had wanted to gag. He chuckled to himself. For a guy who was so open to new experiences, certain things would turn him off faster than he could explain. Like feet. Now rimming on the other hand?

Maybe he should go see if his favorite website had a new release. Some of the guys really got off on rimming, and he loved to see it. He had a few models he enjoyed watching in action, and if he could get some of this tension out of his body, maybe some answers would appear in his mind. Hell, even the thought of it had him getting hard. He really needed to get off, even if his own hand had to do the job. That would require moving, though, and Cade wasn't quite up for it. Maybe after he finished his beer.

Another sigh and he uncrossed his ankles and brought one up to prop on his knee. The movement exposed the hole in the knee of his threadbare jeans, so Cade pulled at the threads and took another drink. Lost in his musings, he didn't realize he had company until a throat cleared at the bottom of the steps.

Cade jerked, and the bottle of beer slipped out of his hand and crashed onto the porch floor. It bounced a couple times and splattered white foam over the steps. "Fuck!" He scrambled to his feet and ran into the house for a towel and a pitcher of water. Rocky stayed at the bottom of the porch stairs, but Cade noticed he'd taken a couple steps back by the time he returned.

He poured the water over the already soaked wood and cleared what would become a sticky mess if left unattended. Rocky took another quick step back when the water came close to splashing on his feet. "Sorry," Cade muttered.

"Didn't mean to startle you. I thought you might have been ignoring me."

Cade huffed in disagreement. "Not ignoring you. Just lost in my thoughts, I suppose."

"Everything okay?"

Not sure how to answer, Cade knelt down and wiped up the worst of the pooling water. He wasn't a big fan of lying, especially since the man who was causing most of his dilemma was the one asking the question. Finally, he shrugged in reply and hung the towel over the rails to dry. "So what's up?"

"Thought I'd see if you wanted that lesson we've talked about. I have some free time this evening and was going to work out. Figured I could show you some of the martial arts moves. If you aren't busy."

Cade reflected for a moment on his need for tension release. It wasn't the kind he'd originally had in mind, but he wasn't likely to get the same benefits from his own hand. Maybe if Rocky put him through his paces first, he could come home and jerk off. Could be a win-win. "Yeah. A workout sounds good. Let me get some shoes on."

He hurried into his bedroom and grabbed socks from the dresser before gathering his shoes from where he'd kicked them off on the floor. When he sat on the bed to pull them on, he glanced up into the bathroom and stared at the cabinet for a long moment. His feet covered, he went into the bathroom and grabbed the small tube of lube he normally used for his nights out on the town.

Cade needed release, more than just the burn of a good workout. The heat between Rocky and him sizzled when they got close, and although he didn't want to go into the night planning on seduction, he wanted to be prepared. He stuffed the tube in his jeans pocket, thankful that they were old and baggy enough to hide the small protrusion. If nothing else, he could see where the night took him, and if it meant coming home to take care of business alone, he would.

They walked back down to Rocky's cabin without speaking. Cade thought about making casual conversation, but he couldn't think of anything to say. Rocky seemed to be having the same issue. He'd opened his mouth a couple times, but when Cade looked his way, he'd snapped it closed again.

Rocky's cabin smelled of man and sweat and even an undercurrent of sex. Cade sniffed the air appreciatively, relieved to know he wasn't the only one jerking off alone around here. It gave him quiet satisfaction to realize that Rocky carried some of the same tension Cade felt.

In fact, Rocky wore the same pair of green shorts he'd let Cade borrow the first night they'd trained together. The pair he'd said were too big. They were, and hung low on his hips, but the long gray T-shirt he had on prevented Cade from seeing anything he really wanted to see. Cade hoped it meant Rocky was fighting an erection just as Cade was.

The hum of arousal filled the air. That undeniable chemistry that drew him to Rocky. The spark, the low burn, the want. Cade felt it all. His breath quickened in his chest to a near pant, and they hadn't even touched. His blood pooled in his groin, stiffening his cock from the mere scent of sex in the cabin.

Rocky bustled around the room, and Cade realized that he knew. Of course he did. They were both wolves. If nothing else, Rocky would be able to smell Cade's arousal. He'd been able to smell it all along, even that first night when Cade had rushed out the door pretending his dick wasn't about to burst.

Cade didn't want to think anymore. He wanted to feel. Needed to put out this fire that left both his mind and body twisted and tangled. He didn't move, just stared. Waited for Rocky to acknowledge him. If Rocky didn't do it soon, Cade would take matters into his own hands, but his instincts told him to wait. Just a minute more.

Rocky fought it. His shoulders stiffened with tension. He barely moved his head and kept his back to Cade. A dangerous choice with Cade as out of control as he felt at the moment. But Cade waited.

Fought it as well. Felt his wolf twitching to be set free. To attack and take what he wanted.

Instead he stood there, stiff as a board, his cock twitching in his faded jeans, until Rocky finally spun around and stalked toward him.

He stopped when they were almost touching, chests millimeters apart. Their gasping breaths mingled. Rocky didn't meet his gaze, kept his gaze locked on Cade's lips, then lower to his chest. Cade's muscles responded, his pectorals flexing in response to that heated contemplation. His nipples brushed against the thin fabric of his shirt and tightened into little buds. Rocky gasped out a breath. The warm air passed through the material and onto Cade's skin.

Rocky leaned forward and nipped the hardened flesh between his teeth, pulling it and the T-shirt out just enough to sting, but not hard enough to really hurt. Cade clenched both hands in his jeans. He wanted to grab Rocky, hold his head in place and never let him stop the incredible torture.

He whimpered instead and threw his head back as his skin sprung tiny goose bumps. His entire body throbbed with want. This was what he'd been waiting for, what he needed. Rocky grabbed Cade's arms, squeezed hard enough that a human would be bruised. He pushed Cade and guided him back until he thumped against the wall.

He finally looked up and met Cade's eyes, then growled out a low warning. Cade got the message. *Stay put.* He didn't have to be told twice. Rocky grabbed the hem of Cade's tank and tore it right up the middle. It hung a bit at the top. Rocky jerked it hard until the fabric gave and he'd bared Cade's chest completely.

Cade spread his legs, needing a little more support before he fell onto the floor. Rocky growled and shoved his hand against Cade's chest. A little grumble of pleasure escaped from Cade's mouth before he could stop it. He'd gone from predator to prey for the first time in his life. The thrill of it had him nearly coming in his pants.

Rocky scraped his nails over the left side of Cade's chest, scoring little lines from his damp nipple to his ribs. He bit the right nipple between his teeth, and this time Cade couldn't hold back his groan.

More. God, don't stop. They were the only words that flowed through his mind.

Rocky seemed to know exactly what he craved. He released the tender bud and nipped his way up to Cade's neck. He bit down with his human teeth hard enough to bruise. *Yes,* Cade's mind screamed. *Mark me. Show them that I'm yours.* Rocky rubbed his body against the front of Cade's, covering him with his scent.

It wasn't enough. Rocky pulled back and flung his own shirt off, then smacked their bodies back together, skin to skin. This time there wasn't a barrier, and Rocky covered every inch of Cade's wide chest with his smaller body even as his mouth continued to suck at the spot on Cade's neck.

Rocky slid his hand up to Cade's throat and pushed his head up and to the side. He held him there against the wall as he licked and growled his way farther up to Cade's ear. His tongue laved the sensitive lobe before he bit down again.

Cade's knees wobbled beneath him, then finally gave out. He started to sink, but Rocky pushed harder against his throat and grumbled a low warning against the side of Cade's head. The vibrations traveled down his spine and his asshole spasmed with want.

Rocky lifted his head from Cade's neck and used his throat hold to turn Cade to meet his gaze. He must have found the answer he needed in Cade's eyes, because he shifted his hands down and grabbed Cade by the front pockets of his jeans. He started to tug him forward, and then he froze. He dug into the pocket and lifted out the little tube of lube Cade had tucked in there earlier.

He definitely had his answer now. Rocky spun him around and grabbed Cade's wrist. Cade stumbled a bit but managed to follow as Rocky dragged him into the bedroom and bent him chest down over the bed. Rocky's weight settled over him. He marked Cade's other side with his scent, rubbing a scorching trail that had Cade bucking up into him. Rocky grabbed his hips and forced him to still, even as he pushed his cock against the crease of Cade's ass and humped against him furiously.

That didn't satisfy him either. He reached below Cade to rip open his fly. Cade raised his hips, and Rocky jerked the fabric down to his knees. Cade heard the brush of fabric as Rocky pulled his own down as well, and the next thing he felt was Rocky's bare skin against him and the thick length of Rocky's cock drilling into his crease.

Cade grabbed the bedding beneath him and clenched it tight in his fists. He tried to spread his legs farther, to angle his hips to get Rocky's dick where he needed it, but Rocky stilled and pushed down into him. His hand roamed up Cade's side to his neck, then over his scalp, where he spread his fingers and held Cade in place. Cade felt hot breath against his ear before he heard Rocky's voice. "Do not move."

Cade managed a small nod against the pressure that held him. Rocky lifted himself off Cade. He heard the thump of Rocky's shoes being kicked off and the whisper of fabric being shed.

Then, finally, the snick of the cap from the lube and a cold drizzle that ran down his crease and over his twitching hole. Rocky's weight came back, and the blunt tip of his cock began to push inside. Cade stilled, waiting for the pain. "Slow," he whispered and felt Rocky's nod of understanding against his back.

He did go slow, waiting for the give as Cade's hole stretched to let the wide head of Rocky's cock inside. Cade buried his face in the mattress as the burn filled him with every inch of Rocky's length. He pushed back against the pressure even as Rocky pushed in determinedly until he was fully buried inside Cade's ass. He traced his hands up Cade's arms and closed his fists around Cade's wrists. He bit down on the unmarked side of Cade's neck and pinned him there, a sacrifice to their desire.

Rocky began to move, short thrusts that tested Cade's readiness. Cade's grunts and moans answered his unspoken question. The lube did its job and slicked the way. Cade's body eased as his muscles relaxed against the invasion. He began to move back into Rocky's slow thrusts.

Rocky took his movement as permission to speed up, just as Cade intended. The teeth left his neck. Rocky trailed his hands up to Cade's shoulders, holding him to the mattress as Rocky began to fuck him as hard and fast as Cade needed. Every pounding thrust pushed Cade into the mattress, his cock rubbing against the bedding in time with Rocky's thrusts. He ached to take himself in hand, a firm grip to bring himself off quickly.

Cade tried to sneak his hand beneath himself, but Rocky wasn't having it. He grabbed Cade's arm and slammed it onto the bed. It didn't take long before Cade felt his orgasm coming without touching himself. "I'm coming. Oh fuck, I'm coming, Rock."

Cade felt the scream of satisfaction building in his chest as his cock hardened and began to jerk. He released the yell even as his prick spewed. Rocky continued to pound into him, keeping his orgasm coming for longer than it would have lasted on his own. When he finished and stilled, Rocky grabbed his hips and fucked into him a few more times. The hot spurt of Rocky's come shot up into him. Cade arched his back to get him deeper. Rocky's trembling body collapsed onto Cade's back, still thrusting through the last waves of his release.

Their gasping breaths were the only sounds in the otherwise quiet room. A few long minutes of just breathing and Rocky pushed himself up and dragged his softening dick from Cade's stretched hole. His spend began to trickle its way down Cade's legs, and Cade twitched at the sensation.

Rocky stood between his legs. Cade could feel Rocky's naked thighs against his own, keeping him spread wide when his instinct was to close his legs. Rocky ran his hand down Cade's hip, across his ass, and into the crease. His fingers dragged through the wet and dipped into Cade's hole.

He twitched and clenched his cheeks together. Rocky chuckled and stepped back. Cade felt his shoes being pulled off, then his jeans being removed. He heard Rocky's footsteps as he walked away, then felt the warmth of a damp cloth when he returned and gently cleaned Cade up.

Cade couldn't move. His body was completely tension free for the first time in... so long, he couldn't even remember.

*C*ade woke up when the damp spot under his chin began to irritate him. He cracked open one eye and realized he'd drooled all over the comforter. Among other things. His body ached in that pleasant, well-fucked, relaxed way. At some point, Rocky must have coaxed him farther up onto the mattress, because only his feet remained dangling over the edge. Cade didn't remember moving.

It took a bit of effort, but he lifted his head and turned it the other direction to see Rocky lying beside him on the bed. He winced at the soreness but couldn't help the silly grin that spread over his face.

"You okay?" Rocky asked between the wince and the grin, and he let out a quick breath of relief when he saw Cade's expression change.

"Yeah. Better than okay. You?"

Rocky didn't answer. He stretched out a finger and traced it over the lingering bite mark on Cade's shoulder. "I didn't mean to be so rough with you."

Cade shivered at the touch. "I'm not complaining."

He pulled his hand away from Cade's body and rested it between them.

"Big day today," Cade said to break the weird silence.

"Yeah."

Cade waited for him to say more, but Rocky remained quiet.

"You want me to go?"

Another long silence and Cade pushed himself up. Rocky reached out and grabbed his arm. "No."

Cade settled back onto his stomach and laid his head on his crossed arms.

The silence grew, and with it the tension began to build. Cade waited. He'd learned last night with Rocky that, if given time, Rocky would come through. Like a champ. Cade's ass twitched. Maybe he could get him to come again.

"My alpha is coming today."

Rocky sounded guarded. Cade didn't understand why. Maybe he just didn't want his alpha to know he was involved with a wolf from another pack? Or another man? Could be either.

"He'll be here for the celebration?"

Rocky scowled. "Yeah, you could say that. And the reparation, of course. I'm sure that's what he's looking forward to most."

The word caught Cade's full attention. He pushed himself up on one arm. "Reparation? What reparation?"

Rocky shrugged. "I thought Gray told you. I offered reparation after Simon's kidnapping. Gray accepted, and my alpha is coming to deal with it."

Cade could tell from Rocky's dead tone that there was much more to the story. "Why?"

"Why what?"

"Why do you have to offer tribute? What did you do wrong?" Cade knew Gray well enough to know he didn't take offers of reparation lightly. He'd said before that it was another part of the archaic system of the Council, but he respected it by taking penance from pack members in his own way.

Rocky snorted and rolled over onto his back. "What did I do? You were there, Cade. You know what I *didn't* do. What a joke. I just stood there while you guys were in danger. That asshole Thomas nearly killed Simon and attacked the alpha, and I just stood there watching the whole thing. Some security expert I am."

Cade couldn't really say anything to refute Rocky's claim; he'd thought the same thing the night of the attack. He knew Rocky better now, though, and considering his omega status, Rocky had no business being there that night. Cade wasn't supposed to know that little tidbit, which made it harder to figure out how to navigate his argument.

"Rock, you aren't here as an expert in battle. You're here to keep the compound safe. That night... well, we were all out of our league. Cormac saved us all, if you want the honest truth."

Rocky shrugged a bit, and Cade wanted to find a way to wipe the hurt look off his face. He didn't know what to do or what to say. He reached out his hand and laid it across Rocky's stomach, offering his silent support. It was really all he had.

"Anyway, it's going to be bad. I just wanted you to know. I still have a lot of shit in my head that I need to work out, but last night helped." Rocky traced his hand over Cade's where it rested against his abdomen. "You sure you're okay?"

"I'm fantastic. Don't worry about me. You aren't the only one who got something he needed last night."

Rocky smirked. "That was fucking fantastic."

"Or fantastic fucking. Whichever." Cade chuckled and winced as his sore muscles protested. "Man, I need to shift and go for a run to work the kinks out."

Rocky cracked up. "Kinks, huh? Yeah, I think we've got a few of those worked out."

Cade reached up and tweaked one of Rocky's nipples. Rocky gasped, and his eyes darkened. "That we do. But not now. I've got a ton to do today to get everything set up for the party. You'll be around, though, right?"

"Yeah. I'll be here."

.   .   .

139

After his early morning training session with Cormac, Simon's brain fogged for several hours until he recuperated. The complexity of the spells continued to deepen, and Cormac pushed him at a fast pace to get him prepared for his big day. That the big day was today didn't seem to matter. He'd treated the morning as he had the rest of the week, joining Simon for his morning meditation, then putting him through his paces.

Part of Simon wept with exhaustion, while the other part thrilled knowing that all of their training would come to fruition with the spell later that evening. The final mystery would be solved, at least as far as his mage status was concerned. He'd been waiting for years for this moment.

Simon paused for a moment to send a grateful thank-you to his grandfather's memory. As hard as it had been to lose him, his journals and memories had brought Simon to where he was now. Had brought Cormac into his life. Without his vampire relative, Simon wouldn't be able to take this last step.

The only bright spot to the end of the training sessions was Riley's excitement in seeing him. Their bond deepened with each day they spent together, and even now as Simon rubbed his aching head, Riley ran toward him and leapt into his arms. Maggie had kept the boys occupied for the most part while Gray worked in his office and Simon trained, but the moment Riley saw Simon, he dropped what he was doing to be at Simon's side.

Simon carried him into the living room as Riley jabbered on about his morning. Apparently, they had made chocolate chip pancakes, which was fun, and cleaned up, which was not fun. Riley realized he didn't have Simon's full attention and gave his hair a little tug to pull Simon's focus back to him. "Simon, can we go outside and play?"

Simon untangled Riley's fingers. "It's not nice to pull hair, Riley. But sure, we can go outside. Let me get a drink first, okay?"

"Okay!" Riley grinned and ran upstairs to see if Garon wanted to come outside too.

Maggie had the kettle heated on the stove, so when Simon went back to the kitchen, he was able to pour a much-needed cup of herbal tea without waiting on the water. He gave her a quick hug of appreciation and laughed when his stomach growled. The smells coming from the oven tantalized his senses.

As usual, Maggie knew his needs before Simon did and handed him a plate of fruit and cheese. Simon took a quick bite of his snack while he waited on Riley to come back. "Anything I can do to help?" His stomach gave a little flutter as he thought about all the preparations going into the party that night.

"Not yet. I'll need a few extra hands later, though."

"Can do. Riley wants to go outside and play for a bit. I'll get him back in, and we'll feed the boys lunch. Then I'm all yours."

"Excellent. Some of the other pack members are coming by later as well. We'll have a party no one will soon forget."

"Have I mentioned how much I appreciate you helping with all this?"

"Once or twice." She laughed. "Simon, you do realize that it's an honor to do this for you and Gray, right?"

He shrugged, and she gave him another quick hug. "Gray is my alpha, but he's also my nephew. I adore him, and I'm thrilled that he found his mate. And speaking of Gray, he's upstairs with Garon. I think our boy is a little nervous about the Council members arriving this afternoon."

"Join the club," Simon grumbled. "I'll go hang out with them once I let Riley burn off some steam."

She nodded and turned back to the stove just as Riley came running into the kitchen. Garon didn't want to play outside, so Simon followed Riley out onto the porch, where he stripped and shifted in the blink of an eye. His mountain lion form bounded around the yard and pounced on every leaf and shadow in his path.

Riley seemed to not only need to shift a bit more frequently than the wolves did, but he also liked to play outside in his mountain lion form while the sun was out. Simon had researched, using the limited resources available, and hadn't come up with any real reason for Riley's constant requests to shift, but Cormac had summed it up pretty simply—wolves were nocturnal; cats were less so. He reminded Simon of the images of lions in Africa, lying out in the baking sun, and it made more sense. Feline shifters were more connected to the sun than their lupine counterparts, so they preferred to shift when the sun was high in the sky.

The cub in Riley exuded pure joy as he played and rolled around in the grass. Simon needed more of that emotion in his life, and watching Riley play helped the lingering pain in his head dissipate into nothing. After about thirty minutes, though, Simon called Riley over. "Okay, Riley. Time to shift back. We need to go inside and help make lunch."

Riley rolled over onto his back and threw his paws over his eyes. Simon had to fight back a grin. "Come on, drama kitty."

Riley peeked over his paw and shifted. He laid on his back in the yard and pouted up at Simon. "I don't wanna go inside."

"I know, but we've got to." Riley's big brown eyes were nearly impossible to resist. Simon tried to stay firm. Gray had let him know he couldn't give in to Riley's every whim. As Gray had obviously raised Garon to be a well-behaved boy, Simon tried to listen to his advice. He should have warned Simon about how difficult it would be.

Riley stuck his lip out, and it might have quivered a bit.

Simon faked a cough so he could cover his mouth to hide his laughter. "No pouting. Let's go. Move it."

With a very long and drawn out sigh, Riley went onto the back porch and pulled his clothes back on. "Sometimes I wish I could stay a lion forever, Simon. It's more fun. I can climb trees and run fast, and I hear better and see better. Being a plain old boy is no fun."

Simon dropped down onto one knee. Riley leaned in and hugged Simon. "You know, I think it might be fun as well. But I'd really miss talking to you. That's a good thing about being a boy, you know. And giggling." Simon gave Riley's ribs a little tickle and got the sound he wanted to hear.

"Yeah. I'd miss you too. I guess I can do it."

Simon scooped Riley up and carried him inside. When he saw that Garon had gotten out a board game and was setting it up on the table, Riley scrambled out of Simon's arms and ran over to see if he could help. Simon glanced into the kitchen, and Maggie waved him back to the table.

"I've got this. You go play with the boys."

"You sure? I'm happy to help."

"Positive. Keep them occupied and out of my hair." She laughed and he joined in. Garon tended to ask a lot of questions when helping out in the kitchen. With Riley added into the mix, the two turned into chatterboxes. None of them minded answering the questions, but a little peace and quiet never hurt either.

Gray joined them a few moments later. He worked around Maggie, gathering the fixings for sandwiches, then joined Simon, Garon, and Riley at the table. By the time they had the game set up, Gray had lunch in front of the boys and was working on making his and Simon's plates.

Sparks of excitement jumped between them every time their eyes met. From the moment they'd woken up that morning and Gray had rolled over onto him for some good-morning loving, the happiness in Simon continued to grow. Gray sensed every time his nerves got the better of him and showed up with a soothing touch or a whispered word through their mind-link. Simon treasured the reassurance and let it calm his anxiety.

Simon returned the favor. Gray's nerves were a bit on edge as well due to the imminent arrival of the Council. They had a laundry list of problems, and any one of them could have irreparable consequences. In a few hours, they'd know for sure where they stood.

For now, they ignored their worries and enjoyed playing with the kids. As usual, Garon trounced them all, but they laughed throughout the game. Gray took Riley up for a quick nap and the other three got to work in the kitchen helping Maggie. They carried food from their house over to the recreation hall, where the party would be held. Gray got held up over there talking to some pack members, so Simon and Garon returned to their house and got back to work.

The hours flew by, and before Simon knew it, Maggie was shooing them both out of the kitchen to go get ready. Garon grumbled a bit but went to put on his dress clothes, while Simon corralled Riley and got him into the tub. By the time he had Riley scrubbed and dressed, Gray had returned. They went to their room to get themselves ready.

When they were alone, Gray pulled Simon close and held him for a long moment. "Everything okay?"

Gray shrugged. "Not sure. Rocky's alpha arrived while I was at the rec hall. I don't like the man. Don't trust him."

"Then we'll be on our guard."

"The look he gave me was full of venom. I'm worried about Rocky, but the reparation is unavoidable."

Simon wrapped his arms more tightly around Gray. "You explained it to me. I don't like it, but I understand. I hope he doesn't hurt him."

"I doubt he will, at least not here. It would break our code for him to bring negativity to our mating celebration. I worry for Rocky when he leaves here. His alpha is full of hate."

"We'll keep an eye on him. There's nothing we can do about it right now. Let's get ready for this party."

"Sounds good."

They shared looks through the mirror and sly glances over their shoulders as they began their preparations. Simon showered first, and Gray stepped in behind him just as he was finishing. He brushed a quick kiss over Simon's lips before Simon stepped out and dried off. By the time he finished dressing, Gray had showered and was trimming the edges of his beard.

It took Gray a moment to realize Simon wasn't wearing an outlandish shirt, as was his custom. He'd found a deep blue dress shirt that he said reminded him of Gray's eyes and sentimentally bought it. Gray smiled, then uncovered his own shirt from the shopping bag it was in.

The shirt matched Simon's green eyes. Simon laughed and Gray pulled the shirt on. Simon helped him with the buttons and turned to work on his hair. He felt that familiar tingle of magic that said someone was mind-speaking to Gray, and Gray turned to him and held out his hands. "The Council members are here."

Simon felt a little weak in the knees, and his heart rate sped up a bit. Gray raised his hand and kissed his knuckles. "No worries. I'll go deal with them. You finish here and meet me downstairs, okay?"

With a brief nod, Simon agreed. Gray kissed his hand again and left the bedroom. Simon forced his attention to the mirror and wished for the first time that he could hear through walls.

17

ocky flinched when he got the message from Gray to come to the main house. The time had come to face the music. Alpha Malone had arrived earlier than Rocky had anticipated, and he knew what was coming. Having been away from his own pack so much on business, he'd grown soft.

He'd especially let his guard down over the past few weeks with the High Moon Pack. He went up to the rec hall as fast as he could and worked on stiffening his spine as he went. His couldn't let his alpha see how weak he'd become, and he did not want to keep either of them waiting. Simon's birthday party was only hours away. Gray needed to focus on handling the Council members and not his reparation.

He forced his thoughts of regret deep into the back of his mind and tried to keep his expression neutral. Alpha Malone waited on the front porch of Gray's house, the deep anger in his eyes not hidden from Rocky. He didn't let Gray see the look he sent Rocky's way.

Gray stood at the door, and Rocky bowed his head to both of them from the bottom of the steps. "Rocky, this isn't the best day for this, as you know, but your alpha wants to handle this right away to make peace between our packs."

"I understand, Alpha Gray. Thank you for your understanding."

"You've been an asset here. When this is done, we are at peace. Do you understand me?"

"Yes, Alpha Gray."

"Alpha Malone, I'd appreciate it if you'd take your discussion somewhere more private. With everything going on tonight, I'd rather not have this business impact the celebration."

"Not a problem, Alpha Gray. This is a personal matter between Rocky and our pack now. I'll see you at the celebration."

When his alpha turned back to him, Rocky could see the gleam of greed in his eyes. Rocky turned and led the way back down the hill toward his cabin. Once they were out of sight of the buildings, his alpha grabbed Rocky by the arm and dragged him into the woods.

Rocky could have broken free of the hold easily, but he knew the consequences if he did. He allowed himself to be spun around and slammed against the trunk of a towering pine. The thick layers of bark cut into his back, stinging as a piece embedded in his skin through his shirt.

"You seem to have failed to mention the mountain lion pack. Did you not consider that to be news I needed to hear?"

Rocky tilted his head to the side in submission. Alpha Malone huffed and rejected him. Rocky flinched, unable to hide that little bit of emotion.

"You will pay for that, omega. Now is the time to tell me anything else you've conveniently forgotten. I have plans in place to take over this pack, and I will not let your negligence ruin them. You will finish your job with this fucking travesty of a pack because I will not allow it to be said that a member of my pack didn't keep his word. And when you get done with this job, you will report back to our pack where you belong. You have some lessons that clearly haven't been learned, boy."

Rocky nodded. The rumble of uncertainty that crept through him couldn't hold back years of training. "Yes, Alpha."

"Tell me what you know."

Rocky struggled to find words that would appease his alpha without betraying a pack he'd come to respect. "About what, Alpha?"

"This pack, what else, you idiot? God, I don't know why everyone says you're so fucking smart. I don't see it."

"Sorry, Alpha. The pack is strong. Gray is a strong leader."

"See, you just proved my point. You think he's a strong alpha? Mated to a mage?" Malone snorted and slapped Rocky across the face hard enough to snap his head back. "He's thinking with nothing but his dick. This is what you think is strong? Damn, I've taught you nothing, boy. This 'alpha' you think is so great is destroying his pack, slowly but surely."

Malone wrapped his hand around Rocky's neck and squeezed. "He's going against the Council and against all of our traditions. Do you think our history means nothing? That our rules are there just for show?"

Rocky shook his head, his hands coming up to pull against the hand choking the breath out of him.

"That's right. Remember your lessons and remember your place. When you get back, you'll get your punishment for this. I refuse to do what needs to be done to you and ruin the party. The Council will be here, and they need to see this pack the way it really is. I should ban you from attending, but they might question that, and we can't have that, now, can we?"

"No, Alpha."

"Once the Council sees what a joke Gray is, they'll remove him from leadership. This pack is just waiting to be taken over. And I plan on being ready to step up and take charge when the opportunity arises. Our pack will grow stronger. We've grown too large as it is. I need to give some of the boys a chance to fight for the right to become Alpha of their own pack. Maybe I'll see who takes you down fastest? Nah, that's no challenge." He laughed at his own joke and shoved Rocky away from him.

"Now, tell me what I can use against him. You had to have seen something. Let me put a little bug in the Council's ears and move this thing along a little faster."

Rocky faced his alpha's wrath if he said nothing, but his thoughts were muddled over everything he'd learned since he'd been with the High Moon Pack. He fought back those lessons and said what his alpha wanted to hear: a gay alpha, a mage, a werelion cub. A laundry list of items that could be held against Gray.

Some bit of himself kept Rocky from spilling too much, and he only related things that his alpha could easily learn on his own just by hanging out with other members of the pack for a few minutes. It was still fuel for the fire, but maybe his words wouldn't do too much damage.

Rocky hunched over and caught his breath for a minute as his alpha turned and walked away. He started back to his cabin to shower and change for the celebration and caught a glimpse of Cade a bit farther down the path but fought the urge to call out to him. No, he needed time to get his head straightened out before he joined the rest of them up at the meeting hall.

He hadn't been forbidden from attending the festivities, so maybe there would be some way he could help. If it didn't work, he'd literally be fed to the wolves of his own pack. Part of Rocky didn't mind. A small part of him was ready for it to be over.

Gray smoothed the front of his dark green dress shirt as he made his way down the steps to his office. The Council members had arrived with an hour to spare before the celebration. He left Simon up in their bedroom to finish getting dressed and went to deal with all the issues currently facing his pack.

The three Councilmen sat in his living room talking quietly. They stood in greeting when he entered the room. Gray bowed his head respectfully. All the werewolves standing before him were men he'd known his entire life. His father considered both Stephen and Phillip close friends. Howard's son Bradford was one of Gray's friends.

At the very least, Gray believed these three men would give his issues the consideration they deserved, without judging him before they stepped through the door. Stephen stepped forward first. Gray felt the power of the man, even before they shook hands. Stephen's white hair and slate-gray eyes personified Gray's idea of an elder, and Gray knew the wolf inside the man could back up his powerful image.

Phillip shook his hand next, and his smaller frame seemed in direct opposition to the other two Councilmen. In this case, his looks were deceiving. As their hands joined, Gray acknowledged that Phillip was one of the strongest wolves he'd ever come across. That power had never been more apparent to Gray than now.

Howard stepped forward last, and instead of shaking Gray's hand, he pulled him into a quick one-armed hug. "I hear congratulations are in order."

"Yes, sir."

"Bradford wanted to come along, but his mate is expecting their first cub any time. He didn't want to leave."

"Completely understandable. I remember that time well."

Howard ran his hand over his bald head and patted Gray's shoulder. "We've much to discuss, Alpha."

"Yes, sir. Shall we go to my office for more privacy?"

All three men followed Gray as he led them to the office and shut the door. Gray pulled his chair from behind the desk, and they arranged the other chairs in a circle. "Where to begin?" Phillip asked with a quick smile.

"I suppose at the beginning. Has the Council uncovered any new information regarding the demon attack?" To Gray, the attack continued to be the most concerning issue. With no leads or clues to go on, he depended on the Council's resources to find some answers.

"Unfortunately not," Stephen answered. "Although we did find an occurrence from about fifty years ago where a wolf was found drained as you've described. At the time, it was treated as a rogue encounter with a demon, since no other incidents were reported. We've also considered a number of missing wolves cases over the years, but have no proof that they are connected to this in any way."

Gray squeezed the arm of his chair and fought back a growl of frustration. "This can't be the first time this has happened. It seemed so organized and so methodical."

Howard nodded his agreement. "Our question is where the mage learned of his spell to drain powers. No one seems to have an answer to that, and we aren't getting any response to our queries from the Conclave of Mages."

"No surprise there," Phillip grumbled. "That group keeps to themselves, and they claim no knowledge of Thomas's spell. We agree with you, Gray, that he had to get the information from somewhere. What does your mage have to say about the matter?"

"He doesn't know either. Simon is still an apprentice and has limited knowledge of the other mages. He has been isolated from the others since his training began. Thomas drained him of his powers as well, as I reported, but upon Thomas's death, the power returned to Simon."

All the Councilmen shared a look before Stephen spoke. "Have the mages not inquired about their missing apprentice?"

"Not once." Gray shook his head. "It makes no sense. If one of ours were caught up in something like this…"

Phillip chuckled. "As you are, Alpha. And yes, when a member of a pack is caught up in something out of the ordinary, our Council takes avid interest. The mages have not, however. This is puzzling."

"Which brings us to the matter of your mating," Howard said. "You realize that you've gone against a long history of tradition by taking the mage as your mate?"

"I do. However, I haven't found anything in our law that states that the mating was forbidden."

"You're correct in that," Stephen replied. "It's not forbidden, but I think our forefathers assumed it would never happen."

"It wouldn't have under normal circumstances." Gray leaned forward and met each of their gazes in turn. "I didn't seek Simon out, but once he became part of our lives, I realized I wanted him to remain with us. With me."

Howard smiled at Gray and shook his head. "Our mates tend to sneak up on us when we least expect them. Are things going well?"

"So far. A few members of the pack are hesitant, but no one has made a formal complaint to me about my choice. Simon won over many of them when he returned the cubs to the pack. When he risked his own life to save my son's, that eased the fears of many of the others. My pack supports me, and my choice, even if they don't all agree with me one hundred percent."

"As it should be," Phillip acknowledged. "You have the respect of your pack, Gray. That's the highest honor a pack can give its alpha."

"Thank you, sir. I do everything in my power to be deserving of that honor."

"The Council has asked us to take stock of the situation tonight at the celebration. We'll be speaking with most members of the pack, but if all is as you say, the Council has decided to not take action at this time."

Gray let out a long breath. "That's wonderful news."

Howard leaned forward. "The key phrase there is 'at this time.' The Council fears that the mage has an unnatural sway over you and this pack, and if we find that to be true, then we will be forced to take action."

As much as Gray wanted to argue, he knew it was the best outcome he could hope for. "Understood."

"And now to discuss the mountain lion cub." Stephen shook his head and crossed his legs. "The mountain lions are different from us, as you know. Their leadership is disjointed, to say the least."

"The lions want nothing to do with the cub and feel that he should be put down to prevent the spread of whatever caused the death of his pack," Howard added.

Gray couldn't stop his growl from emerging this time. The arm of his chair began to snap under the force of his grip.

"Settle, Alpha. The Council doesn't agree with them and has decided to allow you to keep the cub under your protection as long as he's found to not be tainted."

"He's not tainted."

"We will be making that determination as well."

The grim expression on Phillip's face sent a chill down Gray's spine. "How?"

"At this point, we will simply question the boy. Learn what we can about his pack and the attack." Phillip leaned forward, and his eyes locked on Gray's. "I know that he's just a child, but we have no clue what happened there or what the ramifications of the slaughter of his pack are."

"I understand. We've questioned him, but Riley only knows that his mother told him to run and pointed him in the right direction. It's fortunate that he found his way to us."

Howard crossed his legs and leaned back in his seat. "Precisely. Very fortunate. A little too fortunate, perhaps, considering the events that have gone on in this pack."

"Either way," Phillip said, "we will do our best to determine that he has not been corrupted in some way by these attacks."

"He hasn't been." Gray met their eyes, each one in turn. "Between Simon and Cormac, they would recognize unfamiliar magic. I would sense anything in regard to his shifting abilities."

"Ah yes, the vampire. You never do things halfway, do you?"

Gray shook his head. "Cormac is Simon's family. As much as it makes us uncomfortable to have another type of magic in our pack, I believe that these alliances will only strengthen us."

"We shall see, Alpha. This experiment of yours is going to be closely watched."

18

*C*ade stormed through the woods on his way to his cabin, his mind wrestling with the conversation he'd just heard. Rocky had condemned their pack, Gray, and even Riley. This was the man he'd let fuck him last night? The man who'd marked him? And Cade had all but rolled over and begged to be claimed by a traitor?

He punched the outside wall. The sharp stab of pain in his knuckles trailed up to his shoulder. The bruising that still remained from Rocky's bite the night before twinged in pain, and the reminder was exactly what Cade didn't need. Rocky had even pinned Cade against the wall the same way his alpha had pinned him against that tree, by the neck, his throat pulled taut in submission.

He'd submitted. Cade. Strong man. Gray's trusted friend and adviser. And he'd rolled over and begged for a man that would sell them out so easily. A man Cade thought he could trust. He thought he'd been mistaken about Rocky, that he'd misunderstood.

And Cade fell for his act, convinced himself that Rocky wasn't the same asshole he'd first met who'd questioned Gray's every move and couldn't see past his own prejudice. Cade stared down at the blood dripping over his fingers, at his dark skin, now torn and disfigured.

Rocky probably only saw his color as well and thought Cade was lesser somehow because he was different too.

Fuck that. Cade had fought against those fears his entire life. He wouldn't let anyone get away with treating him like some piece of meat to be used at will and tossed aside. He wouldn't give up information about his pack or let someone betray them for their own benefit. He wouldn't let anyone hurt his pack. He'd die first.

Cade stalked up the porch and into his cabin. He slammed his front door so hard the window panes threatened to shatter. If he hadn't left the rec hall when he did, hadn't taken the shortcut through the woods so he could get changed and get back to finish helping with setup for the party, he never would have heard the words that shattered his illusions. Oh, and he'd come along just in time. Rocky whimpering and acting all weak and pathetic.

"Oh no, Alpha. They're bad," Cade mocked. "Yeah. I'll show you bad."

Cade thought he'd finally found something worth fighting for. He couldn't have been more wrong.

No, that wasn't true. He had his something. His pack, his alpha, and their family. It was what he was good for, after all. The side of muscle that took care of problems. And he'd take care of this one as well. He owed Gray that much. Owed it to himself too, for allowing himself to be so fucking stupid.

He might not have the brains that Gray and Liam had, but he had the ability to take care of this problem. He already knew he could kick Rocky's ass in wolf form. Cade snorted to himself. Omega, his ass. Yeah, Rocky might be considered weaker as a wolf, but in the conniving department? Alpha. Cade wouldn't make the mistake of trusting him twice.

He showered and changed into a black dress shirt and black pants. The attire fit his mood more than the celebration he would attend, but he'd look nice for Gray and Simon and put on his happy face. They would need to know about Rocky's betrayal. But not tonight. Tonight, they deserved happiness. Cade would make sure he took any obstacles out of their path to happiness to make sure they got it.

Back out the door in less than five minutes, he was waiting at the bottom steps of Rocky's cabin when Rocky emerged from the woods. Rocky gave a guilty start when he saw Cade, then eyed him appreciatively.

It fueled the fire of Cade's anger even more. Rocky stopped several feet away, finally realizing that this wasn't the trusting fool he'd seduced the night before.

Cade closed the distance between them, his features set in rock-hard determination. The rage that burst through him threatened his very fragile hold on his hard-earned control. "You need to leave. Now. Pack your shit and get the fuck off our compound."

"What?" Rocky staggered back several shocked steps and stared at Cade.

"You heard me. Get out."

"Cade, come on. If this is about last night, I thought—"

"I'm not playing, Rocky. You need to get out of my sight, right now."

"Why? I don't understand."

Cade choked on a bitter laugh. "Why? Because you don't belong here. I thought you did, but you played me for a fool. What, was I just another source of information for you and that prick you call alpha? God, I'm so fucking naive."

"Cade, no. That's not... I didn't..."

"Don't lie to me. I heard you. You want to help him take over my pack? You've lost your damn mind if you think I'm going to stand by and let that happen. You think because Gray mated Simon, that makes him weak. No, Simon makes him strong."

Rocky stepped closer. Cade couldn't hold back his growl of warning.

"You can't just pretend like the problems facing this pack don't exist, man. You have a mage, a vampire, and another breed of shifter roaming freely among your pack. That's real, and you're acting like nothing is wrong. The Council isn't going to let all those challenges slide. It's stupid to act like throwing aside our traditions, our law, isn't a big deal, and you aren't a stupid guy."

"No, Rocky, I'm not. But you are. Stupid, and narrow-minded, and we have no place for someone like you here. You think what Gray is doing is so wrong? Fine. Leave. I thought you'd changed. Hell, I actually just thought I'd read you wrong at first. But I didn't, did I? You're still the bigot I took you for in the beginning."

"Cade, it's not like that. We put the pack first. That's all I'm saying."

Cade snorted out a half laugh. "Yeah, Rocky. That's all you're saying. You know what, do you think it's easy being the only Black man in my pack? Since my folks left to stay with my brother-in-law's pack, I've been the only man here without pearly white skin. Do you think it was easy growing up and knowing I looked different than the rest of my pack? It wasn't. But you know what Gray taught me? That it didn't matter. He never saw the color of my skin, never once judged me for something I had no control over."

"It's not the same thing."

"Yes, it fucking is the same damned thing. You judge people like you have the right. So what that Gray is gay? I didn't see you minding when you shoved your dick up my ass last night. Was that just another form of your bigotry? 'Fuck the Black guy, why does he matter?'"

"Cade, no. Stop. It wasn't like that."

Cade pushed Rocky back and then followed. "So fucking what that Simon is a mage? He's fought more for this pack than you ever have. And now you want them to get rid of Riley like he's some piece of trash? He's a kid, just a fucking kid, and so fucking what if he's a mountain lion? It makes no goddamned difference except to assholes like you."

"He shouldn't be here, Cade. That's all I'm saying. It's dangerous for the pack to mix like that. Think about all our traditions. We're supposed to stay with our own kind. There's a reason for that."

Cade didn't even stop to think. A red haze of fury covered his eyes. He threw back his fist and punched Rocky as hard as he could. Rocky's head flew back. He stumbled before regaining his balance and throwing up his arms in the same defensive posture Cade saw that first night he'd battered the black bag hanging inside his cabin. Cade swung again, but this time Rocky blocked his arm and pushed back against him.

"What the fuck?" Rocky rubbed the spot on his jaw where Cade's fist had connected. Cade hoped he'd broken it. He wanted to break him in half and was half tempted to shift and do just that. He restrained himself, barely.

"I told you to get out of my sight, and you just wouldn't shut up. Do you think I don't know your little secret? I do, you asshole. I figured it out. You're an omega, and you're so fucking scared that someone will find out. Well, I found out, and I don't care. You think that just because you're weak as a wolf, you have to be stronger as a man. I hate to break it to you, but you just proved that you're the weakest man I know. You can't even fucking think for yourself. You have to believe every old-fashioned bit of tradition that comes your way. Well, Rocky, you're an omega. You want me to treat you like one? Huh? Is that what you want? You sure as hell bent your neck for your alpha when he told you that you were nothing. He was right. You are nothing. You just proved it to me. Now get the fuck out of here before I shift and break your neck. That's all omegas are good for, isn't it?"

Cade stormed away, afraid if he kept going he really would do what he'd threatened. He needed to find Gray and let him know what was going on, but he didn't want to interrupt the festivities. Tonight should have been for celebrating, but instead Cade felt like his world was crashing down around him.

He struggled against his emotions for the entire walk back to the rec hall. Still shaky, he went around the side of the building and leaned against the sun-warmed wood as he tried to calm his temper. He heard footsteps approaching and stiffened. If Rocky had followed him, Cade swore to himself that he would shift and end it right now, regardless of the consequences.

Instead, Maggie rounded the corner of the building. She took one look at him and stopped. "Cade?"

"Hey, Auntie." Cade took a deep breath, determined not to let her see how upset he was.

"What's wrong?"

Hell, he couldn't hide anything from her. He'd never been able to since he was a kid and stole the last of the brownies from the kitchen one summer when they'd been hanging out with her. She'd called him on it then, known exactly who it was that had done it.

Cade turned and hit the side of the building with his undamaged fist. A matching pair, not unlike the damning bite marks on his shoulders. She laid her hand on his back. Her quiet strength began to calm him.

"We need to be on our guard," he finally whispered to the smooth pine planks. He couldn't risk looking at her; he might break down, and right now he needed to be strong and in control.

"Should I get Gray?"

"No. We can handle this. Rocky and his alpha are going to try to turn the Council against us so they can take over the pack leadership."

"The fuck they will!" Her indignation set him at ease. He wouldn't be alone in this fight, after all.

"There's more." He hesitated to reveal Rocky's secret for a moment, but he wasn't aware of the implications. Maggie probably was. "Rocky is an omega."

"So?" she asked.

He looked away from the wall and finally met her gaze. "Um, so I don't know. But I figured it out. It seemed like a big secret, so I wasn't sure how significant it was."

"Not a lot. My mother was an omega. It's really just a label to identify members of the pack who need a little additional training in wolf form. But…"

"But?"

"If Rocky's from an old-fashioned pack, they still treat omegas like garbage. My mother told us about some of the hate she'd experienced growing up, but I haven't seen much of it still existing. It doesn't surprise me that ignorance continues to be passed on through generations. Does Gray know?"

"I don't think so. I didn't tell him. I… I should have."

She reached up and laid her hands against his cheeks and forced Cade to meet her eyes. "Don't do that. Don't get that haunted look in your eyes. You didn't betray Gray. I know how your mind works, boy. I've known you since you were in diapers. You haven't had that look in your eyes in years, and I'll not let it come back now."

"I shouldn't have kept it from him."

"Why? It wasn't your secret to tell. Rocky should have declared his status when he arrived. Gray knows the traditions; he'd have known what to do. Rocky chose to keep that secret. You, my dear, will always put Gray's interests first. I don't doubt that, and neither does he."

Her words helped, but Cade knew he'd talk it over with Gray as soon as he could. He hated that little feeling of doubt, but now wasn't the time to confess. They had a party to get to, and a visiting alpha to put in his place. And if Rocky dared show his face, there'd be an omega right beside him.

*S*imon stepped down the stairs, uncertain what the reaction would be once he reached the bottom. Gray stood in the living room with the members of the Were Council, but there didn't seem to be the towering wall of tension he'd expected. One of the Council members had a hand laid over Gray's shoulder and his mate's head was tossed back as he laughed.

Simon waited by the door, but his attempt at reading the situation simply confused him. The crisis he'd dreaded for days slipped away as he viewed the apparent support Gray was receiving from the visiting wolves. He cleared his throat, and all eyes turned to him. Gray waved him over, so Simon switched on his smile and walked to Gray's side. He slipped his arm around Gray's waist. Gray pressed a kiss to the side of his head before turning back to their visitors.

"Simon, I'd like to introduce you to Stephen, Phillip, and Howard. Councilors, this is my mate, Simon Osborne."

"Good evening. Thank you for coming."

Simon shook their hands in greeting, and the next several minutes passed in a blur of friendly conversation, with only a hint of the grilling he'd expected. It was more of a "meet the family" type questioning than a "sit in a dark room under a spotlight" interrogation. He felt they sincerely wanted to know more about him, and if some of them dug a little deeper than was polite for a typical first meeting, Simon didn't allow the questions to bother him.

Phillip seemed the most determined to get answers from him. The older man exuded power unlike anything Simon had felt before. It was as if Simon could trace the magic inside the man and see his wolf begging to be set free. He shivered at the thought of going up against this wolf. His mate was strong, but Phillip was stronger.

The current questions involved his interactions with the demon. The fact that the demon had been able to drain magic from the cubs troubled all of them. "So, explain your abilities to me again. You could actually *see* the magic?"

"It's not quite that simple, but yes. Different mages have different ways of describing their power. For me, it's visual. Most of the spells I'd seen during my training were blues and greens; this one was reds and blacks."

"And you knew by the color alone that the spell was bad?" Phillip's confusion had turned to genuine interest.

"Yes. Imagine you're facing a strange wolf. If you see that its fangs are bared and its hackles raised, you know it's a threat. Spells are the same for me. I see the red and black, and it shows me the snarling and growling of the magic."

"That makes sense. And you were able to save the cubs by turning the demon's magic on itself?"

"No. Actually, I just confused it for long enough to free the cubs and get the hell out of there. I'm not a fighter, but I wasn't just going to leave them there."

Howard and Stephen stopped their conversation with Gray to listen in. Gray returned to Simon's side in a show of support. "Simon had never fought before, but he went in there single-handedly and rescued our cubs."

"Incredible," Howard murmured.

"Not really," Simon answered. "Look, they were kids. I wasn't going to leave them there to die, shifters or not. I knew it was forbidden and chose to face the consequences. I don't regret my actions. In fact, I've gotten so much more in return."

"And that, my boy, is what being in a pack is about." Stephen nodded and turned to the others. "I don't believe we have time for a more in-depth conversation at this point. We have a celebration to attend."

Simon's stomach trembled a bit but this time from good nerves. He wanted to answer as many questions as the Councilmen had to ask, but they wouldn't be able to iron out any real details in a short conversation anyway. The time to head over to the rec hall had arrived.

Gray yelled up the stairs for the boys, and they trampled down the stairs a minute later. Riley froze when he saw the strangers in the living room and hustled his way to Simon's side.

Garon, as alpha-heir, greeted the Council members with a level of seriousness and respect that made Simon proud. He may not have had anything to do with raising Gray's son to this point, but his heart swelled with the maturity Garon showed. Then Garon glanced over his shoulder, caught Simon staring, and made a silly face.

Simon and Riley both burst into laughter, drawing everyone's attention. He just shook his head and scooped Riley up in his arms. Simon realized the night would be a little tough for Riley and wanted him to be as comfortable as possible. When they walked into the rec hall and caught everyone's attention, he didn't want it to upset the little guy. Gray and Garon joined them, and Gray wrapped his arm around Simon and another over Garon's shoulder.

"Riley," he whispered. The little boy raised his head from where he'd hidden it in Simon's neck. "I know we talked about this, but remember that you can stay with us all the time. Me, Simon, Garon, and Aunt Maggie will all be there, and so will Liam and Cade. So if you get worried, just find one of us, okay?"

Riley nodded. "But you won't leave me, will you?"

"Nope," Gray said and laid his hand on Riley's back. "Simon has to go to his meeting with Cormac after we're there for a while, but Garon and I aren't going anywhere."

"Okay."

The group left Gray's house and went to the celebration. Simon couldn't stop smiling. He and Gray had left most of the planning to Maggie, at her insistence. She wanted their opinions, and then wanted them to get out of her way so she could get it done. They didn't mind at all. Simon and Gray agreed that they didn't want the room turned into a weird high school prom reject with balloons and streamers, but other than that, they hadn't had much opinion on the subject. There were other, more important things to think about.

That didn't mean that the night itself wasn't important, and as they walked in, Simon realized that the transformation of the rec hall itself mirrored the changes in his life over the past few weeks. It was the same old room, polished up and lit with the soft glow of candles and twinkling lights.

Hurricane lanterns sat on white tablecloths in the center of each table. Each held a white pillar candle, and the base of the glass was surrounded by vines of ivy. The buffet table sat in its usual spot at the front of the hall, but it, too, was covered with linens. Instead of the usual crockpots and plastic bowls, silver tureens were filled with steaming offerings.

His nose detected the scent of buttery lobster, and Simon wondered if Gray's alpha salary was enough to cover such extravagance. He still had so much to learn about his mate.

Beside him, Gray let out a happy sigh. "Perfect."

"Yeah. They did an amazing job. Who is the florist?"

"Oh, that's Roger's wife, Lynne. You remember the guy who played the guitar?"

"Of course, how could I forget him?"

Gray laughed. "Yeah, he's pretty unforgettable."

"I'm hungry." Riley eyed the food-laden table with a gleeful expression.

"Me too. We need to wait a little bit, and then we'll eat, okay?"

The Council members also looked around the room in appreciation. "Wonderful job, Gray."

"I can't take the credit," he said. "This is all my Aunt Maggie's doing."

Phillip smiled at the mention of her name. "And how is Magdalene doing these days?"

Her voice answered from behind them. "Why don't you ask her yourself?"

After another round of introductions and hugs, Maggie turned to Gray, Simon, and the boys. "Why don't you guys mingle a bit while we finish setting up?"

Gray nodded, but before they could move away, Garon stepped up to her. "Aunt Maggie, that's a lovely frock you're wearing."

"Frock?" Gray mouthed the word to Simon, who fought back a smile.

He's been spending too much time with Cormac, Simon answered in mind-speak.

"Why thank you, Garon."

And she did look lovely. Her dress was dark purple velvet, and she'd swept her hair up into an intricate knot. Simon watched as she fussed over Garon and Riley, then turned her attentions to Gray. They hadn't discussed the fact that Gray's parents weren't able to attend, but Simon knew Gray wished they could be there. Maggie's presence soothed that ache a little.

He'd briefly considered inviting his own, but they probably wouldn't have come anyway. Or if they had, it would have just been to make an appearance because they felt they had to. Eventually he'd have to introduce them to Gray, but that was a task for another day. Today, he just wanted to bask in the glow of the welcome he'd received from this incredible group, try not to worry about the inquisition committee behind him that watched his every move, and then, in a little while, go out into the woods with Cormac and become a full-fledged mage.

Just an average night.

Gray and Simon stuck together as they toured the room and greeted everyone. Simon received lots of birthday well-wishes and a few sly presents, even though he'd specifically requested none. They finally sat down to eat with the boys on either side of them. The low hum of voices drifted through the room. Simon looked around at them all with a huge grin on his face.

His eyes skipped over the Council members discreetly questioning one pack member after another. He could tell by some of their gestures that the Councilors were getting an earful. Gray leaned over, nuzzled his ear, and whispered, "Eat."

Simon nodded and took a bite and continued watching. He spotted Cade sitting back in the corner, his face an unusual mask of indifference Simon hadn't seen before. He stared until Cade felt his gaze and turned his way. Simon smiled and Cade returned it, but he looked quickly away.

Simon followed the direction of his eyes and realized Cade was keeping an eye on Rocky's alpha. No one had paid much attention to the other wolf, although no one seemed to be directly rude to him. Nevertheless, after a few moments of the visiting alpha speaking with any of their pack members, the pack member would make their excuses and leave him alone, usually shaking their head or rolling their eyes.

Rocky—Simon looked around the room for him again—wasn't there. Simon worried about the reparation and what exactly it meant in their culture, but he didn't want to ask. He would, later, and he'd see that someone looked in on Rocky to make sure he was okay. In fact, he'd ask Cade. There'd been a definite something going on between the two for the past week, even though Simon hadn't pinned either one of them down long enough to be nosy.

A little throat cleared beside him. Simon turned to see Emma standing next to his chair. "Hello, Emma. You look beautiful."

Her little golden curls had been primped to perfection, and she wore a yellow dress with flowers and ribbons. Emma spun around so he could get the full effect, and Simon nodded. "Gorgeous."

"Thank you, Simon. Mommy let me pick my dress myself. I didn't want pink."

"I think yellow is perfect. It matches your hair."

"Yeah. I thought so too. Simon, Mommy said I couldn't ask you to dance with me." She raised a little brow and looked at him with such an air of expectation that Simon couldn't help but grin.

"I suppose that's because she knew I would want to ask you to dance first."

She grinned back and blushed a little. "Oh."

He leaned over and whispered in her ear. "I suppose I have to dance with Gray first, but I'd be honored if you'd be my second dance."

She giggled and nodded before running off to find the rest of the kids to play. When everyone finished eating, they cleared the tables and moved some of them out of the way. Roger settled in the corner with his guitar and started strumming. Everyone turned to Gray and Simon, and they led the way to the end of the room.

Gray must have made a pretty speech. Simon half listened, but mostly he just looked around the room and smiled at each and every smiling face he found. By the time everyone started applauding, Simon felt so full of joy he could barely contain himself. And then he was in Gray's arms, their foreheads pressed together as they swayed in time to the music. A verse or two into the song, a few other couples joined them.

The song ended, and as promised, Simon sought Emma out in the crowd. He scooped her up, and they spun around the floor a few times. She babbled in his ear about finding an alpha of her own one day. Simon had no doubt she would.

When he dropped her off at the edge of the dance floor, he found Cormac waiting there for him. "It's time."

Simon let out a sigh and turned to meet Gray's eyes. *Love you,* he heard through their link. *See you in a little while.*

Love you too. And this pack. So much. He left the rec hall behind Cormac, only turning back once to watch them all in the glittering lights.

20

*W*atching Simon leave with Cormac raised Gray's hackles in a way he hadn't anticipated. His mate. *His.* Possessiveness had never been a big issue for Gray, but now? He wanted to pin Cormac to the wall and demand his submission.

A small hand brushed against his. Gray looked down to find Riley standing next to him. Riley stared at the door Simon had just walked through with the same irritated expression on his face Gray was sure was on his own.

Alpha. Father. Mate. All of Gray's roles merged into one maelstrom of conflicting emotions. He'd never had mixed priorities before taking a mate. Even his son fell under the same guidelines as the rest of the pack. With Simon, his immediate family felt more nuclear. Protect Simon and Garon, protect the rest of the pack. Hell, even Riley added another layer of confusion.

Gray ran his hand over Riley's hair. The cub looked up at him with worried eyes. "How about some cake?"

Riley smiled, but it was halfhearted at best. "Okay. Is it chocolate?"

"Yeah." Gray winked. "And I'll get you a piece with extra icing."

The promise got him a brighter smile, but Riley's gaze kept drifting back toward the door. He led Riley over to the dessert table and helped him pick out a piece of cake, then took him over to the table where Garon and the other kids sat eating.

Gray stood behind them for a moment, one of his hands on each of their shoulders. He looked around the room at the rest of his pack. He could smell trouble in the air and feel it in the darted looks he received from several members of the pack.

Liam and Cade stood at opposite ends of the room. Neither appeared happy. With a nod, he had Liam start his way. Gray left the boys' sides and went to Cade. Something was bothering Cade. Gray could see it on his carefully neutral face. Having known the man since childhood, Gray knew a faked expression when he saw it.

The corner of the room where Cade stood was quieter than the rest of the room. Liam joined them a moment later, but Cade didn't meet either of their eyes. "Cade?"

Cade raised his face and pasted on a smile. "Congratulations again, Gray."

"Thank you. Now what's on your mind?"

"I'm fine."

Liam huffed. "Yeah. Fine. Sure you are. Now tell us the truth."

Cade glanced to Alpha Malone and back to Gray. "I'm concerned. He's stirring up trouble."

"No surprise there." Gray shrugged. "I have the Council's support."

"Maybe not. I heard Malone talking to Rocky earlier. He wants to take over the pack, and I think he's going to challenge you."

Gray laid his hand on Cade's shoulder, mirroring his earlier action with the boys. "Let him try. I'm more than capable of taking him."

"I know." Cade let out a long breath and looked around the room. "I guess I'm worried about the damage he's going to do in the meantime."

Liam leaned in and grinned. "Divide and conquer time, boys?"

Gray laughed, and Cade rubbed his chin. "You know, that just might work."

"It always used to."

During their teenage years, the three of them had gotten into trouble multiple times. No surprise, really. Three rambunctious teenage werewolves? Not much could have kept them out of it. But they'd been clever. Or at least they'd thought so at the time. Gray's dad never fell for his crap, but he had a soft spot for Liam.

If they wanted permission for Gray to do something, Liam would ask. Gray and Cade did the same with the other's parents. They usually ended up getting what they wanted. Liam had nicknamed their scheme the divide and conquer, and whenever they had something big going on, they used it as code.

Gray looked around the room at the unsettled faces, though there weren't many, and watched the Council members as they mingled and asked their questions. His focus returned. He was alpha of this pack, and they were hurting. Being alpha was about more than kicking ass, although if Malone tried any bullshit, Gray would be more than willing to oblige.

He sent Liam left and Cade right. Gray took the middle. All it took were a few words and reassuring touches. He followed in the wake of the Council members and made sure everyone knew he wasn't threatened.

Maggie caught on to their scheme and left the table where she'd settled with several of the older women. In some unspoken agreement, she and the other ladies began circling the room as well.

Divide? No. They weren't going to be torn apart by this. Their pack would be okay.

As would his mate.

Gray made his way to Roger and leaned in close. "Got anything that'll perk this place up a bit?"

"Oh, I'm sure I've got something that'll do the trick."

Gray nodded and left him to it.

The music started a couple minutes later, and smiles began to form on previously tense faces. Several of them sang along and tapped their feet in time to the guitar.

Gray circled around and ended up on the opposite side of the hall from Alpha Malone. The other alpha's anger couldn't be hidden. He seethed. Phillip stood beside him, clearly as disgusted with Malone's attitude as the rest of them.

He walked away.

Gray stared Malone down. This was his home, his pack, his family, his life.

Malone stared back. The power and tension between them built. Gray didn't back down. He wanted Malone to make a move, dared him to. Malone looked away first and dropped his gaze to the floor. For now, Gray had gotten his wish. The other alpha backed down, unwilling to make a scene in the midst of the party.

"That's right. Mine." Gray's grim reminder to himself settled his mood further. He continued his way around the room, making time for everyone until he made his way back over to the boys.

Garon looked up and smiled. Riley grinned, and Gray had to chuckle at the chocolate icing smeared all over his mouth. Yeah, things might be rough, but nothing was coming between them. Gray would make sure of it.

He grabbed a napkin and cleaned up Riley's face. Everything would be just fine.

Simon had debated with himself over the course of the past week as to where he wanted to do the mystery spell on his twenty-fifth birthday. The sentimental side of him wanted to do it back at his grandfather's cabin, in the special circle his grandfather created in the garden. The practical side of him thought it would be more prudent to stay close to the party so he could get the spell over with and get back to the celebration.

Cormac left the decision up to Simon, and in the end, his practical side won. They set up a new circle out by the pond where they'd first found Riley. It wouldn't be quite as powerful as the one his grandfather had created and used for years, but it would serve. As they walked through the dark woods, Simon became more grateful that he'd made the decision to stay close. It felt right to do this here, at his new home, and away from the negative connotations attached to the old circle, where Thomas had betrayed his trust.

As much as Simon wanted to rush to the location and get the spell done, he found himself dawdling as they drew closer. His nerves began to overtake him, and his heart began to race. Fear of the unknown sent him into a panic attack. Simon leaned against a towering pine, the scratchy bark against his face as he tried to get his breathing under control.

Cormac was several steps ahead before he realized Simon had stopped. He turned and hurried back to Simon's side, his presence neither soothing nor heightening Simon's state. Simon took deep breaths as Cormac looked on, and finally raised his head enough to meet Cormac's worried gaze.

"I'm okay," he mumbled. It didn't sound convincing even to his own ears.

"Simon, you are okay. I know you're worried. You have every right to be. But you also know how important this step is, and I wouldn't do anything to harm you."

"I know, Grandfather. I'll be okay."

Cormac placed a hand on Simon's shoulder. Together they walked the rest of the way to the clearing. They'd prepared a simple circle out of smooth rocks. Simon had taken the time to focus positive energy on each stone as they'd put it in place. Cormac stepped immediately into the circle and sat down with his legs crossed.

Simon walked around the circle, focused on each rock and the protection it provided. He called his power to him and let the colors of the night wash over him. He thought of Gray, his strength and determination. He ran his hand over the dark blue of his shirt and smiled at the notion that they'd each worn something the color of the other's eyes on the day of the party.

The memory helped him settle his nerves, and he drew strength from deep inside himself. Gray had faith in him, and he would find it in himself.

"Let's do it," Simon said as he straightened his back and forced himself to join Cormac inside the circle. They sat facing each other with their knees brushing together. Simon held out his hands, and Cormac laid his on top.

"Clear your mind, as we've practiced. Hold your center and let our magic merge and mingle. I'll take care of the rest."

They'd actually practiced this a couple other times as part of Simon's training. He hated the thought of letting anyone else through the layers of protection he'd formed. Thomas had stolen his trust along with his magic. Simon did trust Cormac not to do the same, but part of him still feared the outcome.

As they'd done in practice, Simon lowered his shields enough to let Cormac's magic join his own. He judged that magical presence and let his magic decide that it was safe. When his magic deemed Cormac's intent pure, it allowed him further inside. Learning to trust his magic had been difficult for Simon, and he still wasn't one hundred percent there. The one time Cormac had, with prewarning, tried to remove a piece of Simon's magic, he'd felt the difference immediately and had been able to shut it down.

Simon concentrated on the different colors of light he could make out in his mind. He'd also learned that darker intent came with a darker color. Cormac didn't see the magic inside himself the same way and explained that each mage had their own way of determining the types of magic that surrounded them. In Simon's case, "good" magic meant light colors of green and blue, while darker magic kept toward red and black.

This spell appeared more white than anything else. Simon's mind interpreted the difference as one of neutrality. The spell was neither good nor bad. It simply was. As Cormac's magic touched each section of his mind, Simon's magic responded. He could hear Cormac muttering the words of an ancient spell, but the words weren't important. Simon knew that somehow and concentrated on the results.

The colors inside him grew, expanded. Simple green became multiple shades. The same with the other colors. More appeared, shades of yellows and oranges Simon had never seen before. There was even some red and black, but the colors didn't have the menacing feel of the magic he'd seen Thomas use.

Simon laughed at the sheer joy. As each new window opened in his mind, the rush of new magic flowed through his body. If he hadn't felt the hardness of the ground beneath him, Simon would have thought he was floating. Cormac squeezed his hands tighter, grounding him, but Simon could feel through their connection that Cormac felt the same excitement of the power flowing between them.

"It's so beautiful." And enlightening. The subtle differences in the colors began to clarify in Simon's mind as different shades of power. Some good, some not, but all necessary. He could feel the windows opening, just as Cormac had described. The magic filled his mind and expanded in ways he'd not been able to imagine.

As he drifted through the phases of his mind, letting the incoming magic solidify in ways he could only begin to understand, Simon heard a sudden shout. A burst of anger and fear that shocked him.

At first, he thought he was absorbing something else from Cormac. He opened his eyes and stared across the circle, but the vampire didn't appear to be in any distress. "Grandfather?"

Cormac opened his eyes, and Simon could see the swirling colors in them. He appeared almost drunk with the power flowing between them. The intrusion wasn't coming from within the circle. It was his connection with Gray battering at his shields.

Simon turned his focus to his mate and heard shouted words. He jerked his hands from Cormac's grip and scrambled to his feet. Cormac yelled at him, but Simon's mind was already backing away from their connection. Cormac grabbed his arm before he stepped out of the circle.

"Simon, we're not done. You can't leave."

"We're done. The pack is under attack." He stepped out of the circle, his magic fluttering wildly around him. Simon started to run, gathering his strength and forcing his guards back up as he hurried back to the compound. Cormac joined him in moments, his vampire speed allowing him to easily catch up.

"West gate. Go."

Cormac hesitated for a moment, but he must have seen the determination in Simon's eyes because he picked up speed and was soon out of sight.

The swirling colors created a mirage effect as Simon ran, making it difficult for him to concentrate on his path. He tripped several times but managed to keep his footing. He'd never heard Gray sound so panicked, not even when Simon had contacted him when the demon's magic was draining Garon.

Whatever had caused his mate to shout, Simon needed to be there. He had to help.

21

*A*fter his argument with Cade, Rocky considered packing up and leaving. He could send someone else from his team in to finish the last of the security setup. It only needed a few final adjustments as they began putting the system to use. He could go back to his pack and face the reparation he had coming, then heal up and move on to the next job.

He couldn't do it, though. Not yet. He needed to settle things with Cade, even if it meant another fist to the face. He had to at least explain what Cade had overheard, get Cade to see he wasn't out to get Gray. This pack meant everything to Cade, and thinking that Rocky had betrayed them had hurt Cade deeply. Rocky had never imagined Cade having such a fierce temper, but witnessing it firsthand had pushed Rocky closer to Cade instead of further away.

In a strange way, seeing that deep passion in Cade, that unwavering loyalty, settled Rocky in his decision. It might not matter much after what Cade had overheard, but Cade's defense of his pack had done more to solidify Rocky's resolve than anything.

The party for Gray and Simon continued going strong up in the recreation hall, and Rocky wanted to at least make an appearance and wish them well. As much as he didn't understand their mating or the risk Gray was taking to mate with someone who wasn't pack, he did want the alpha to be happy. And yeah, he wanted Simon to be happy too. The guy didn't have a mean bone in his body, and if anyone needed what a pack could provide, Simon did.

Family. He'd never felt that sort of love from his home pack, or any pack for that matter, but there were moments when he had witnessed it among the others. The longing to belong would fill him up and spill over into some outward action. He'd step too close to a conversation, smile at the wrong moment, and end up with his ass kicked.

That didn't happen here. No one feared Gray. They respected him. Rocky figured they all knew he could kick their asses if he needed to, but he never did. Gray didn't have to rule with an iron fist. Not like Rocky's alpha, who would beat the crap out of you first and ask questions later.

Gray wasn't on a power trip. He didn't need to be. Gray knew he was strong and so did his pack. Rocky shook his head to clear away his confusion and started up the steps to the rec hall. By the time he reached the top, he just wanted to look in and catch one glimpse of them smiling and happy.

The windows were thrown open to let in the cool night air. The sounds of talking and laughter rolled over Rocky as he stood on the outside looking in. Gray stood in the center of several pack members, holding a laughing Riley in one arm. He must be telling some fantastic tale that involved him waving his arm around crazily because everyone was cracking up.

Other pack members sat at tables, and they all seemed so damn happy to be there. Rocky continued looking around the room until he finally caught a glimpse of Cade. He sat in a corner, leaned back in a chair, and looked like he didn't have a care in the world. Rocky could see the lines of tension in him, the tightness in his huge arms as they crossed over his chest. He watched as Cade's hand crept up to his shoulder and rubbed the spot Rocky had marked.

Without stopping to think any further, Rocky went into the hall and started for Cade. Their eyes met. Cade dropped the legs of his chair back to the floor and began to stand.

Rocky froze and gave Cade a moment to get his defenses in place. This wasn't an attack, and he wanted Cade to know he wasn't coming after him. Cade took a couple of steps toward him, but he didn't seem as angry as he had been before. That was good. Maybe they could talk this out after all.

Rocky's phone vibrated at his hip, and as tempting as it was to just smack it into the off position so he could keep moving, he had responsibilities. He snatched the cell from its holster and flipped it open.

He had a new text—from the compound's security alert system. The perimeter had been breached. Rocky's stomach lurched, and he looked up to meet Cade's puzzled expression before taking off at a run back out the door. He heard Cade's thudding footsteps behind him. Raised voices came from inside, and Rocky heard Gray's voice shouting orders. Gray had received a text as well, just as the system was designed to do.

Cade caught up with Rocky at the bottom of the steps and grabbed his arm. Rocky spun around, bracing instinctively for a fist that wasn't there. Cade stepped back, his eyes wide.

"I'm not going to hit you again. I'm sorry. What's wrong?"

Rocky shook Cade's arm off and pulled his shirt over his head. "The perimeter has been breached. West gate."

Without a word, Cade ripped his tie off and shifted before Rocky could even think to catch up. His clothes landed in a pile behind him as he tore out toward the west gate. Another wolf leapt over the edge of the balcony, followed by several more. Rocky jerked his pants off and leapt like Cade had taught him. He landed on the ground several feet away in wolf form and took off after them.

He stayed behind them by several yards, but amazingly kept up. The wolves in the lead were already by the gate, and a snarling fight began as wolf met wolf. Yelps and howls filled the air. Rocky slid to a halt. Cade already had another wolf pinned by the neck.

One of the intruding wolves tried to sneak past him, and Rocky snarled and batted it back. Another member from the pack attacked it from the side. Rocky looked around at the battle. The High Moon Pack members were outnumbered but holding their own.

Something was wrong. Rocky's gut screamed at him, his instincts demanding he figure it out. In the time it had taken them to get the alert, shift, and get out to the gate, the invaders should have been farther onto the property. Rocky froze. His eyes drifted back to the center of the compound, then back to the fight.

He caught Cade's wolf eyes again, then turned and ran back the way he'd come. He heard Cade's outraged howl behind him but didn't stop. This time he wasn't frozen in fear. He needed to get back to the others and didn't have a way to let the pack know. He wasn't a member of their pack and couldn't communicate with them. No way was he giving any information to Alpha Malone. His alpha would find a way to use it against them.

No, he had to get back and find out what was really going on. The most vulnerable pack members were at the compound. Rocky didn't know where Gray had sent them, but they couldn't have made it far. There were too many of them to disperse quickly. Too many kids to round up and manage. And Rocky… he couldn't leave them alone, unprotected. Gray would want him to go back and help. Some part of Rocky shifted, a piece of his mind that he'd held locked away, frozen in fear. He wanted an alpha like Gray. He wanted a pack like theirs, even if he didn't deserve it.

Minutes later, he made it back to the bottom of the rec hall steps and looked around. He could smell something, a burnt sulfur type of stench that flooded the area. It smelled so bad it made it hard to concentrate on his other senses. Rocky couldn't hear anything, and there weren't any other wolves around that he could see.

Then he heard a child's scream. He raced up the stairs and leapt through the screen covering one of the windows. A man stood in the center of the room. His streaked black-and-gray hair fell halfway down his back. One arm extended toward a few pack members who appeared to be unconscious in the corner. The other reached out to Garon and Riley, who huddled together behind a table and a wolf Rocky didn't recognize.

The wolf growled at the strange man, a low threatening sound that would scare off a lesser man. This guy didn't bat an eye. In fact, he laughed it off. Rocky didn't know who the wolf was, and he didn't stop to try to figure it out. It didn't matter. The wolf was protecting the kids, and Rocky would do what he could to help.

His entrance caught the stranger's attention, and the man spun around and glared. He assessed Rocky in one withering glance. "They sent an omega?" He laughed and revealed long fangs. A vampire.

Rocky snarled, and the vampire shifted. A large black-and-gray wolf appeared in his place, already moving for Rocky.

Fuck. He didn't know vampires could shift. He was in so far over his head. Cade's words drifted through his mind: he didn't have to be the strongest or the fastest. Just stronger and faster. This wolf was twice his size, but Rocky was faster as a man.

The vampire-wolf leapt, and Rocky shifted. His foot swung up and struck the wolf across the jaw. It stunned him enough that he slid several feet to the side. Rocky spun around and put himself between the wolf and the cubs. The other wolf moved up beside him, and they formed a barrier of protection between them.

"Garon, call your dad, buddy. We need Cormac and Simon." He tried to keep his voice calm, but the boys were terrified. Riley started toward Rocky, but he held out his hand to stop him. "Wait there, buddy. It's going to be okay."

The vampire-wolf snarled and shifted back to his human form as quickly as Rocky had. He held out his arms, and Rocky felt the pull of magic. He remembered a lesson of Simon's, one he'd overheard when he was working that he hadn't thought twice about at the time. He'd filed the information away in his mind in case he ever came across another mage. Mages could control humans, but not their animals. Rocky hoped the same held true for vampires or whatever this guy was.

"Boys, shift. Now!" he yelled and began his own transformation again.

The vampire screamed in frustration, and Rocky leapt, tackling him to the ground. He tried to get a grip on the man somewhere, using his powerful jaws to his advantage. The vampire hit him across the head and prevented him from taking a bite. The man tossed Rocky aside, stronger than any human should be. But he wasn't human. He had the vampire's strength and the ability to shift. Rocky landed against a set of chairs, and they all fell against him with a crash. The vampire started for the boys again, and Rocky scrambled to untangle himself. He leapt again as the other wolf attacked the man from the front.

He got a chunk of the vampire's leg in his mouth but couldn't hold. The moment he broke skin, a searing pain burst into his mouth. He had to release his jaws. The vampire turned to him again and kicked Rocky across the room. He hit the wall with a thud but rolled to his feet again.

It pissed him off. He hated losing. Fight smarter, not harder. Another lesson he'd learned from Cade. He rolled his neck around, wincing at the sting. *That all you got? My alpha has kicked me harder than that on a good day.*

The other wolf leapt as well, with the same results. It provided enough of a distraction for Rocky to get his wits together. Whatever this guy was, he was too strong for them to take down. The other wolf whimpered as it stood, and Rocky saw that one of its front legs was twisted.

Rocky circled around, and the vampire stormed after him again. Before the vampire could make another strike against Rocky, a gray blur leapt onto his back. It knocked the vampire off balance, and he stumbled to the side.

The little wolf snarled and jumped at the vampire, catching his pants in his teeth. The vampire yelled, and he shook him off. *Garon.*

Rocky had to help but couldn't get a break. He couldn't keep one eye on the kids and fight at his best. As much as he wished he could tell the boys to run, he didn't have the ability. So he took the distraction Garon provided and attacked again. Another bite led to more pain, and the vampire screamed as Rocky got hold of the sensitive skin below his ribs. His fist slammed between Rocky's eyes, once, then again, and Rocky fell to his side.

The injured wolf used the advantage to leap again. It howled in pain as its leg cracked up against the vampire's body. He tossed it aside as well. It slid to the floor and didn't move. At least the man was finally showing signs of strain.

His injuries didn't slow him down enough. The vampire kicked Rocky in the ribs. The bones snapped. He howled in pain, and the sounds were echoed from outside. Garon must have gotten through to his father. The pack was coming, and they were getting closer. Rocky only needed to hold the vampire off for another minute or two and the cavalry would arrive. The vampire seemed to realize it as well. He glanced over at Riley, then at Garon. He smirked down at them. "I'll be back for you."

He shifted, man to wolf again, and ran faster than any wolf Rocky had ever seen. He leapt through the screen Rocky had busted out on his entrance. Rocky listened for a moment to make sure he didn't hear him coming back. The only noises were the howls of the approaching pack. They let him know it was almost done.

Rocky shifted back into his human form and crawled over to Garon's side. The boy shifted back to his human form as well, and Riley crawled over to them in his mountain lion form. He curled up on Garon's lap. Rocky huddled close to them both. Gray and Cade burst into the room, and Gray fell to his knees by the boys.

Garon had a large bruise already forming on his face. Rocky felt like one giant bruise himself. He stuffed his fist into his mouth to keep from crying out and scaring the boys as he tried to roll up to his knees. Large hands stopped him.

"Just lie still," Cade whispered and ran his hands down Rocky's sides. Rocky winced when he hit the ribs the vampire had kicked, and he knew they were broken.

"It was a vampire, Cade. But it could shift to wolf. I tried to stop him. Garon leapt into the fight when the other wolf got hurt." Rocky looked over to where the other wolf lay still on the wood floor. The motion made him dizzy. He saw black spots forming in his mind and took one more glance over to the cubs to reassure himself they were safe before he gave in to the darkness and closed his eyes.

22

*S*imon made the run back to the rec hall in half the time it had taken him to make the walk. The entire time, he cursed his human vision and human speed, both limitations that kept him from getting back to his family as fast as he needed to. By the time he burst through the door, he was gasping for breath and ready to go to war.

The battle had already been fought, however, and the destruction was all that remained. Simon sought out Gray and found him kneeling on the floor with Garon and a shifted Riley. Cade tended to an injured Rocky, and several other pack members attended an injured wolf off to the side.

How bad is he hurt? Simon asked Gray through their mind-link.

He'll be okay. Just some bruises. A nasty burn on his mouth from biting the vamp.

The vamp?

Gray glanced over his shoulder at Simon. It was a vampire that attacked them. A vampire who could shift into wolf form.

Simon tried to digest that information, but it didn't make sense. He ran his hand over Riley's tawny fur, and Riley shivered beneath his touch. The poor kid. He'd just started settling, and now this. The injured wolf to the side caught Simon's attention again.

Who is it? Simon met Gray's eyes, but his mate didn't answer. *Gray? Who is it?*

Aunt Maggie. She tried to protect the kids.

Simon rushed to Maggie's side and squeezed between the pack members surrounding her. He crouched beside her and laid a hand on her muzzle. She whimpered and licked him before she let out a pain-filled yelp and lay still again. Simon used his magic and sent a tendril through her body to seek out the injuries.

Her leg was broken in two places, and Simon found some internal injuries as well. His magic spoke to him, the pulsing red revealing the worst of the problems. His instincts answered. *Gray, I need you to help.*

Gray carried Riley over. Garon walked beside them, a large bruise on his cheek. Gray had his free arm over Garon's shoulder, and the boy huddled close to his father. Simon reached out and held on to Gray's arm. He waited until Gray's attention focused on him.

Is this okay?

Gray nodded in response.

Simon used his magic to connect to that of his mate. *Focus on healing her,* he told Gray as he tuned in to the healing power.

His magic sparkled with greens and golds as it joined to Gray's. His mate's wolf was unsettled, the swirling tones revealing high levels of both agitation and alertness. Simon almost used his magic to calm Gray but decided against it. Gray knew what he needed, and at least on the outside, he appeared calm and in control.

Simon returned his attention to Maggie and the disjointed colors surrounding her wounds. He pushed magic into Maggie's still form, and she began to growl. Gray started to jerk away, but Simon held him in place.

"It's going to hurt a bit, Auntie. Just stay still for me, okay?"

Simon could feel her pain and, after a moment, she slipped into unconsciousness. It was a blessing, really. Her body had sustained so much damage that Simon was afraid to push too hard and put her into shock. This way he could concentrate only on healing her injuries and not worry so much about causing her additional pain.

Behind him, more people came into the hall. Simon heard them gathering around and the low rumbles of conversation. It grew louder and louder. When Simon finally healed her as much as he was able, he turned to glare at everyone distracting him from his task.

The Council members stared at him in shock and confusion. They'd seen him healing Maggie, and his connection with Gray. More trouble, but at the moment Simon really didn't care. He turned to Garon. "Hey, buddy. You need some help too?"

Garon nodded and held out his arm. Mottled bruising covered the upper part of his arm and over to his shoulder. He must have hit something hard to give him such deep bruises. "Can I shift?"

Simon looked at Gray, who nodded his approval. Garon shifted with a wince and, once in his wolf form, he lay down. Simon knelt beside him and ran his hands over the injured shoulder. Gray laid his hand on Simon's shoulder, and the magic shimmered again. Garon wasn't badly hurt, but Simon could at least ease some of his pain. He focused on the bruised shoulder and then on Garon's cheek, where he'd seen marks earlier. When he finished, Garon licked his hand, and Simon stood up to join Gray.

The Council members stood behind him, their horrified gazes switching between Simon and Garon. Simon looked down at himself and realized he was glowing, like he'd done the night his magic first returned after being stolen.

And Garon shouldn't be able to shift outside the full moon at his young age, but there he lay, his wolf settled and his eyes closed.

Rocky's alpha smirked. "Well, I guess we don't have to wonder anymore if the mage being here has impacted the pack. It's unnatural. The boy shouldn't be able to shift, and the mage is messing with their magic. Hell, you could see it. All those weird colors swirling around them. Makes you wonder, doesn't it?"

The Council members didn't disagree, and one of them actually nodded as the other alpha spoke.

Gray began to growl low in his chest. Simon squeezed his arm to quiet him. He'd expected nothing less, but he refused to just sit back and do nothing when he could help heal his family.

Garon huddled in next to Simon and Gray before shifting back to his human form. He leaned against Simon wearily, and Simon's magic took notice of the boy as well. Riley leaned into Simon, and the four of them connected. Simon's magic burst into a shower of sparks, surrounding them all. It took him a minute, but Simon understood that his instincts to protect his family had necessitated a response from his magic. He let it guide him yet again, and he felt a barrier of protection form around them.

Maggie returned to her human form, and his magic quickly covered her as well. Alpha Malone scoffed. "See what I mean? Just look at them. You've got to do something about this. I'm telling you, this will spread, and their magic will infect the rest of us as clearly as it's contaminated them."

One of the pack members covered Maggie with a blanket, and Gray barked out a request for more blankets. Almost everyone in the room stood there naked, and the injured ones needed to stay warm to keep shock at bay.

Simon looked around at the others in the room and saw other injuries and pain-filled expressions. He ignored the conversations going on around them. Phillip stepped closer to them, held out a hand, and Gray growled. Phillip froze and stepped back.

Gray pushed Simon behind him and handed Riley to him. Someone handed Gray a pair of jeans, and he pulled them on. He kept an eye on everyone before turning to gather Garon's clothes from where they lay across the room.

He helped his son get dressed, checking his shoulder and face carefully. "You okay?" he finally asked.

Garon nodded and laid his head against Gray's stomach. Simon could see his shoulders trembling. Gray ran his hand over Garon's back. "It's okay, son. We need to check out the rest of the pack. They need our help."

They moved as a unit to the other pack members, Gray pushing his alpha power out through the room, and Simon feeding that energy with the healing green and gold sparks churning through him.

With the worst of the injuries treated, Simon's magic began to wane. The sense of power that had coursed through him since the interrupted spell faded. He concentrated on re-centering the remaining tendrils.

The room became divided as Simon stood next to his mate. The majority of the pack moved to surround them, leaving just the Council members and Rocky's alpha standing near the door.

Gray kept one eye on them as he walked through his pack, giving each member a reassuring touch until they all settled. He stepped to the front of the group and crossed his arms over his chest.

The Council faced him, and Simon took note of the disconcerted looks on their faces. They'd gone from the somewhat friendly adversaries to the men Simon feared before their arrival.

"Alpha Gray, this display has been somewhat disturbing," Phillip began.

"Our fears have been confirmed," Howard continued as he stepped forward. "The mage has too much sway over the pack."

"I disagree." Gray didn't hesitate in his defense, but Simon could see the tightening in his arms where he held his tension. "My mate was able to heal wounded members of our pack, using my power, not his own. He channeled it and helped." His gaze drifted over to Alpha Malone. "Say what you want, but keeping my pack healthy is a gift, not a curse."

Malone snorted. "Right. I'm sure you'll say whatever you can now. But we've seen it for ourselves. We know. You can't deny it."

Stephen stepped away from Malone and drew Gray's attention. "I hate to agree with him, but this is highly unusual. We could actually see the powers merging, Gray. I've never seen anything like it before."

"That's because there hasn't been anything like the bond Simon and I share before. You're quick to write it off as evil, without even understanding the good it can do. My question for you, though, is who were the wolves who attacked us? I find it very unusual that this alpha, if you can even call him that, shows up and tries to drive a wedge between me and my pack, and then wolves just happen to show up the same night to assist in an attack against us."

Malone sputtered out a reply. "Councilmen, this accusation is ridiculous. My pack is not involved in this in any way."

Howard didn't seem as convinced. "Where did we put the injured wolves who attacked?"

"In the cellar, under the rec hall. I have several members of my pack standing guard over them for questioning. Several of them are mortally wounded. You'll need to speak with them shortly."

Phillip nodded. "I'll handle it." Stephen and Howard nodded their agreement. Of the three of them, Phillip had the most experience in interrogation, and he would be able to get more information from them than the others. He left the room, and the other two Councilmen turned to Gray.

"You understand our concerns, Gray?"

"I do. But I will not say that what you witnessed tonight has anything to do with Simon and our mating. He used his ability to protect us, to heal us."

"I'm sorry, Gray." Howard stepped closer, and his eyes hardened. "I disagree. We can't allow this mating to continue."

Rocky awoke in time to hear the Council members speaking. The conversation continued around him, the outsiders of the pack trying to convince Gray to disavow his mating with Simon. The alpha, of course, refused.

The argument began to grow louder as two of the Council members argued with Gray. Finally, Stephen, the largest and most powerful of them, stepped forward. "This is not up for debate, Alpha. You will separate from this mage and return your pack to its previous status. This cannot continue."

Rocky turned to watch Simon, who paled and held Riley close at each pronouncement. Gray appeared ready to shift and tear them all to shreds. Rocky's own alpha looked smug.

With a low groan, Rocky rolled onto his side and climbed to his feet. Cade started to stop him, but Rocky shrugged his arm away and stepped in front of Gray. "No."

"Excuse me?" Stephen arched a brow, and Rocky's alpha made a grab for him. Rocky stepped to the side and shoved his alpha's chest to get him to back away. There was no mistaking the condescending tone in the Councilman's voice.

"You heard me. I said no. You cannot force this alpha to leave his mate when all you've witnessed is Simon healing injured members of his pack. Is that not the definition of a true alpha-mate, a true complement to the alpha? Someone whose gifts and strengths lie in areas that the alpha himself doesn't possess? Is his power so terrifying to you that you can't see that he makes this pack stronger in ways that we can't even explain?"

The Council members continued to stare at him, and Rocky turned to Gray. "Your mate is a blessing to this pack, Alpha. Please don't let them change that. You have shown me what a true pack is in the time I've been here. You and your mate are a pair to be admired. I'm sorry I didn't acknowledge that sooner."

"Thank you, Rocky. Your support means a lot to me."

Rocky's heart eased. The pain from the way he'd betrayed Gray earlier was still fresh, but the balm of Gray's easy acceptance helped. Rocky turned to his alpha. "I no longer wish to be a member of your pack. I officially withdraw myself, with these Councilmen as witnesses."

He turned back to Gray. "I'd be honored if you'd allow me to join the High Moon Pack. I know others will want to join as well, when word of the good things here spreads. There are others like me who have been forced into packs that don't approve of them and treat them like dirt. My experience will be an asset to your pack, and I give it freely."

Before Gray could reply, there was a snarl from behind him. Rocky turned to protect himself, his arms flying up in a defensive stance. He didn't need to worry. Gray reached out his arm faster than Rocky's human vision could track and grabbed Rocky's alpha by the throat. He had him pinned to the ground and struggling in just a moment.

"He's mine now," Gray murmured. "I'd suggest you take your poison and get the fuck off my property." He threw a glance at Rocky over his shoulder. "I accept. Welcome to the pack. We'll make it official as soon as possible."

Rocky lowered his head. "Thank you, Alpha. I won't be the only one." His gaze moved to the Council members. "I know this is different, that it breaks tradition. But some of our traditions need to be changed."

He sought out Cade and stared into his dark eyes for a long moment. Cade nodded, encouraging him to go on.

"I'm an omega. My entire life has been about hate and fear over something I didn't do. I can't change how I was born, no matter how hard I've tried. This is our tradition. This is our history. Berate the weak. Treat them like shit. Beat them, shame them. These are the lessons I've learned about pack history. It's time for change."

Simon stepped forward and stood beside him. "I don't know what an omega is, but it doesn't matter. You're welcome here." Simon laid his hand on Rocky's arm and looked over at Gray.

Phillip reentered the room and joined Howard and Stephen. "The wolves aren't from Alpha Malone's pack. They're loners but are following a new leader."

Rocky nodded. "That's what we need to focus on. There's a reason for all this, I'm telling you. I don't know about fate and all that, but this pack is under attack from something I don't understand." He shook his head and turned to Simon. "I think whatever that man was, he had all three types of magic. I don't know. I can't feel it like you can, but from the way you described it, I think that's what he was."

"What do you mean?" Phillip crossed over to Rocky. Gray finally released his hold on Malone's throat. He stepped over to Simon and kept himself between his mate and any threat.

"I saw fangs, so I thought it was a vampire. But then he shifted. I thought I was confused, but now I don't think I was. He was using magic on us, I know that much."

Simon nodded. "I believe you, Rocky." He looked around the room. "Where's Cormac?"

Everyone stopped. "I don't know," Gray answered.

Simon paled, and Gray wrapped an arm around him. "We'll find him. Liam," Gray called, but his beta wasn't in the room either.

Rocky turned to Cade, whose eyes had grown panicked at the realization that one of his best friends was missing.

Gray closed his eyes, then opened them a moment later. "He's not answering."

"Where was he last?" Rocky asked.

"Out at the gate with us," Cade replied.

Rocky turned to Gray. "I can try to use the security cameras. See if I can find him."

Gray nodded. "Good. Cade, go with Rocky. If he finds anything, let me know. I'll be out searching."

The Councilmen nodded. "We'll help."

Rocky ran for the house, as fast as his injured side would let him. It wasn't nearly as bad as it had been, and he didn't understand why. Maybe Cade could explain it later.

23

*G*ray gathered a few other pack members and prepared to search for Liam and Cormac.

Simon stepped up beside him. "I want to come too."

"I need you to stay with the boys." Gray leaned in and placed his forehead against Simon's. *They shouldn't be alone right now.*

Simon grabbed Gray's arms and squeezed. I know you're right, but I want to help. What if they're hurt and you need me?

Then I'll get them to you as fast as I can.

Maggie cleared her throat and drew Gray's attention. "I know I didn't protect them before, but I will now. I know Simon wants to go find Cormac."

"Auntie, I don't blame you for what happened. You did everything you could."

Maggie nodded, and her eyes filled with tears. "I'm sorry, Gray."

Gray pulled her close and whispered into her ear. "Don't fall apart on me now. I need you to be strong. We need you."

She nodded against his chest. Gray gave her a gentle squeeze and gestured Simon over. He took Gray's place, wrapping her up tight.

Gray locked gazes with his mate over her shoulder. "We'll be back."

"You'd better be. I love you."

Gray nodded and went out onto the porch. He calmed his nerves as he took his pants off and laid them over the railing. The others trailed out behind him, and within minutes a half dozen wolves stood around him.

We'll head for the gate. Spread out and keep in contact. If you sense anything unusual, contact me immediately.

Everyone took off into the darkness. Gray stayed at the center of the group as they spread out. He called to Liam several times through the link but didn't receive a response.

They were halfway back to the gate when he received his first update. *Alpha, I found a trail.*

On my way, he answered. He raced through the woods and found a couple pack members waiting for him. He could smell Liam and followed the scent deeper into the woods. What would cause Liam to head out on his own when he knew the cubs were being attacked? It didn't make sense.

Liam's scent switched to the bitter tang of blood. Gray slid to a halt. The others stopped beside him, and Gray moved forward cautiously. A strange, acrid odor filled the clearing as well, clogging his senses.

His vision worked fine, however, and the sight of the two bodies lying underneath a tree had him tearing forward again. Liam and Cormac lay beneath the branches of a low pine, their bodies a patchwork of blood and bruises. Neither was conscious.

Cormac's body half covered Liam, like he'd thrown himself over Liam to protect him. From the state of the burns on Cormac's back, he must have done just that. Gray shifted and crouched under the tree. "Fuck. I don't know where to even touch them."

Phillip knelt beside Gray. "Best to get them back to the compound as quickly as we can." He looked around the clearing and back to Gray. "I don't know what did this, but I have no doubt that we aren't equipped to deal with it at present."

Gray nodded and crawled forward. Phillip pushed the lowest hanging branches out of his way, and Gray was able to lift Cormac's body. He couldn't tell for sure if the vampire was alive, but something told him there was still a spark of life remaining.

Phillip gestured behind him, and Howard shifted and came forward to Liam. He squatted beside him and checked for Liam's pulse. Gray held his breath.

"He's alive. Barely. We need to move." Howard lifted Liam, and they started back for the compound.

Gray walked as fast as he was able, trying to keep from jostling Cormac's body. The vampire never budged, not a single twitch or sound. Gray sped up to a half run.

Simon, we found them. They're both hurt badly. We'll need you.

I'll be ready.

They carried Cormac and Liam back to the rec hall. The seriousness of their injuries sobered everyone. No one spoke a single word. The pack, even those with injuries, gathered around them.

Simon rushed over to them. Gray laid Cormac on his side on one of the tables. His dress shirt was shredded in the back, showing his burnt skin. Simon gasped and stretched out a hand to him. Gray held him back for a moment.

"I need you to look at Liam too. They're both bad, but I don't know who is worse."

Simon nodded. Gray grabbed his hand as he turned to Howard, who still held Liam in his arms. "Someone set up another table. Quickly." Several members of the pack jumped to action. Simon walked over to Liam and raised his hand to hover over Liam's head.

"I don't know who to help," he whispered. He looked back over his shoulder at Cormac and then to Gray. "They're both in bad shape."

They placed the table next to the one holding Cormac, and Howard lowered Liam onto it. Simon glanced back at Cormac once more before turning his attention to Liam. Gray felt his magic responding to Simon's as his mate turned on the healing power.

But nothing happened.

Simon frowned and focused harder. He sighed and turned to Gray. "You'll have to try. I think I'm on empty after earlier."

Gray tried to hide his wince but couldn't. Simon looked away from him. "I'm sorry."

Gray laid his hands on Simon's shoulders. "Don't be. We can't expect you to save the world. We handled injuries before you, and we'll do it the old-fashioned way now, okay?"

Simon nodded.

Gray focused on Liam and tried to find the thread of his wolf's energy. There wasn't much there, but he pulled on what he found and tried to force Liam to shift. His beta didn't respond.

The pack members gathered around them, and each one laid a hand on either Liam or Gray where they could.

Maggie laid a hand on each of them. "Try again."

Phillip, Howard, and Stephen stepped behind Gray and placed their hands on his back. "Pull harder, Alpha. You can do this."

Gray focused again, felt the building energy of his pack and the Councilmen as they focused on him and Liam. He found the thread of Liam's wolf again and yanked with all his might.

He roared as he did it, and the yell ended with a howl as his body shifted into his wolf in automatic response. Liam's body responded as well, and where the man had lain on the table, now a gray wolf lay in his place.

So much power flowed through them that it forced the others to shift as well. Gray felt a head push at his shoulder and saw Riley in his mountain lion form looking up at him. He nudged him back, rubbing their heads together for a moment.

Liam's breathing evened out, and although he didn't regain consciousness, Gray knew it was a sign of his healing.

Simon watched as the pack banded together to help Liam, and he'd never felt more helpless. His magic barely responded to him. No one thought to check on Cormac. Simon stood at his side and ran a hand over Cormac's hair.

For once, his grandfather wasn't in perfect form. His face was dirty, his shirt torn and bloody.

Bloody. Simon glanced down at him again. Cormac needed blood. He hurried over to the abandoned food tables and found a carving knife before rushing back to Cormac. With a deep breath, he sliced the skin of his wrist and held it over the vampire's mouth.

No response. Simon pushed his wrist against Cormac's lips, and after a moment, he felt movement. Right about the same time, he heard an outraged snarl beside him.

Gray shifted back and reached for Simon's arm, but Simon pushed him away. "Let me do this."

Cormac made a noise, not quite a growl. He bit down on Simon's arm. Simon hissed in pain and bit his lip.

Gray paced behind him. Everyone else came around as well, forming a circle around both tables. All eyes were on Cormac's mouth where it latched onto Simon's wrist.

Simon ignored them all. He leaned down and put his mouth to Cormac's ear. "Wake up, Grandfather. Come on. Come back to me."

Gray wrapped his arms around Simon's stomach. "Enough."

"Not yet. Just a little more."

Cormac's eyes opened, and he jerked.

"Shh," Simon whispered. "It's okay, Cormac. It's me. You're okay."

Cormac seemed to realize what he was doing and wrenched Simon's arm away from him. Blood trickled down his face, and he covered his mouth with his hand. The movement pulled the burns on his back, and he cried out.

"Don't move. You're hurt. It's going to be okay."

Cormac's eyes cleared, the confusion of moments before beginning to fade away. He glanced past Simon to Gray. "We need to talk."

Gray nodded.

Maggie appeared at Simon's side and wrapped a bandage around his still-bleeding wrist. "What were you thinking, boy?"

Simon pressed the bandage against his arm and didn't reply. He looked at Cormac, and his grandfather nodded a quick thank-you. That was all the acknowledgment Simon needed.

"Liam?" Cormac asked.

"He's fine," Gray answered. He nodded toward the other table, and

Cormac glanced that way. He let out a breath and turned back to Simon and Gray.

"I need to go. But I'll be back tomorrow night." He struggled to sit up, and Simon tried to force him back down.

"Grandfather, no. You're injured."

Cormac covered Simon's hand. "I know, child. And I need to feed. I can't do that here." He turned to Gray. "We should be fine for the night. I saw him, the one who attacked us, and he's wounded. Your wolves got in a few good bites, took a chunk out of his side. It'll take him some time to heal from that much damage."

Simon helped him get off the table. Cormac stood in front of him. He raised his hands to Simon's face. "You're weakened. You tried to save them all, didn't you?"

Simon shrugged.

"Caution, child. You have to be on your guard now. Spend tomorrow with your mate and the cubs outside in the sunshine. Refill your stores as much as you can."

"Yes, Grandfather."

The wolves parted, and Cormac walked out of the room, his head held high and barely a twitch in his step. Simon could just make out the wavering lines of magic around him. Deep reds and black. Dark, angry colors.

He felt a tug against his pants and found Riley standing beside him. Garon stood just behind him. They both looked up at Simon with such needy expressions that he pulled them both close. He crouched down, and they surrounded him and wrapped their arms tightly around his neck.

"Are you hurt?" Riley asked him with a tremble to his lips.

"Nope. Are you?"

Riley shook his head.

Simon stood up and lifted Riley with him. He wrapped an arm over Garon's shoulders and pulled him close. "I don't know about you guys, but I'm tuckered out. Anyone else ready for bed?"

The adults chuckled a bit, although uncomfortably. Gray nodded at him. They all needed rest.

"Councilors, you are welcome to stay with us. It seems we'll have more to discuss tomorrow."

Stephen shared a glance with Howard and Phillip. "We'd appreciate that. Thank you, Alpha."

Simon looked around a moment. "Hey, where did Alpha Malone go?"

Maggie sighed. "He tore out of here like the hounds of hell themselves were after him as soon as you all left to go find Cormac and Liam. I would have stopped him, but… hell, I really didn't give a shit."

Stephen chuckled. "It's fine, Magdalene. We know where to find him."

"And we will be having a discussion with him regarding his treatment of Rocky," Howard added. "Among other things."

"Good. That man was foul."

Gray helped everyone get themselves together. They walked out of the rec hall in a large clump. Simon watched as Gray touched everyone who passed them before leading the rest to their house.

Cade and Rocky were waiting for them in the living room. Rocky had reset the alarms as best he could. Nothing appeared to be damaged, but he wasn't taking any chances. Simon appreciated it. He didn't know if they had the energy to fight another battle right away.

A limping Liam, still in wolf form and barely able to stand, followed them. Simon had felt Gray communicating with him a couple times, but his mate didn't share anything with him. Liam jumped up onto the couch and settled in. The Council members followed them upstairs.

Riley fell asleep in Simon's arms. Gray grabbed pajamas for both boys before turning their room over to Howard and Phillip. Stephen went into the guest room.

Garon stumbled along behind them, half-asleep as well. Gray helped him get his clothes changed and piled him into the center of their bed. Simon held Riley while they got him changed as well, then laid him down beside Garon.

Gray turned to Simon and laid his hands on his face. "We're going to have a talk about you cutting yourself like that. But not tonight."

"It was the right thing to do, but I agree. Not tonight." He raised up on his toes and wrapped his arms over Gray's shoulders. He pressed a quick kiss to his mate's mouth. "Still love me?"

Gray rolled his eyes. "You can't get rid of me that easily. I have a feeling you're stuck with me."

Simon grinned. "I like that plan." He climbed into bed next to Riley. Gray slid in behind him and spooned up close.

Rocky and Cade walked slowly back to the cabins without speaking. The silence wasn't uncomfortable, even though Rocky thought it should be. He rubbed his sore ribs and winced.

Cade stopped in front of Rocky's cabin. "You okay?"

Rocky shrugged. "Not really. Tonight didn't go like I expected."

Cade sighed. "No kidding. What the hell can go wrong next?"

"Let's not tempt fate. At least now we've got a better idea of who, or what, was behind this." Rocky swiped at his mouth, the reminder of the bitter taste of the vampire's blood fresh in his mind.

"You regretting leaving your pack?"

"That's the one thing I don't regret. I'm... relieved? I needed to figure out what was going on in my head. All these differences, changes, I couldn't process. It makes no sense, yet, it makes perfect sense."

"You have to decide your loyalties, then fight for them. That's what this pack is about. What I'm about."

Rocky stopped and turned to face Cade. "I've got a lot to learn from you, if you're still willing to have me."

"Yeah." Cade stared at Rocky for a long moment. "I'm sorry I judged you like I did."

"You had good reason. I'm not perfect, Cade. Never will be. I'm fucked-up and have years of practice at the hands of wolves like Malone who believe differently."

"It won't be easy. Being here? With us? You'll see a lot of things that aren't done like other packs. There are others who believe as we do. It's not just Gray, but our alpha is a good man and a fantastic leader. You'd do well to learn from him."

Rocky chuckled and started up the steps. "You the president of his fan club?"

Cade shook his head. "Yeah. So I admire the hell out of the man, what of it?"

"Nothing. I'm thankful he gave me a chance. I won't let him down. I'll do my best not to let you down either."

Cade followed Rocky up the steps and leaned in close. "All we can do is try, right? See what this is and where it leads?"

"Yep." Rocky smiled and reached out for Cade's hand. They went into the cabin together and straight to the bedroom. Cade stripped off his jeans, the only clothing he'd managed to put back on. Rocky did the same.

Rocky pulled the blankets back and crawled into bed. He collapsed on his uninjured side and huffed. Cade didn't move, and he cracked open an eye to see what he was doing.

He stared down at Rocky with a look that Rocky had never seen before. Fear, hope, confusion. Everything rolled into one mess that had him scowling. Rocky pulled the covers back on the other side and patted the mattress. "Stop thinking so hard."

"I just... I don't..."

"Cade, shut up. Get in bed. Please."

He complied and settled on his side, facing Rocky.

"Tomorrow is soon enough, okay?"

Cade nodded. "I'm sorry. I need to say that now."

"I am too. And thank you."

"Thank you? Why?"

Rocky reached out his hand and traced it over Cade's head to the still-visible mark on his shoulder. Cade trembled when he brushed his fingers over it.

"For believing in me, for teaching me about the kind of wolf I could be."

"But—"

"No. Stop. You knew my secret and didn't use it against me. Hell, you didn't even judge me like every other pack who figured out my omega status."

Cade slid a little closer and pushed their foreheads together. "I know about being different. Maybe we're just different enough for each other?"

Rocky half smiled. "Maybe so. I'm willing to give it a shot, if you are. I'm not leaving until this is over, I can promise you that."

Cade nodded, and Rocky angled his head to press their lips together. Rocky leaned in closer and tucked his face into the corner of Cade's neck. His breath brushed over the bite mark, and he gave it a quick lick. Cade arched his neck in response.

Rocky's body responded immediately to the gesture. He nipped the skin, and Cade trembled beneath him. He wanted nothing more than to bite down and put his mark on Cade permanently. His heart pounded in his chest as he continued to tease the spot that would make it forever.

Not yet, he decided. Cade deserved more than a quickie after the night they'd had. He wanted to give Cade what Gray and Simon had earlier that night. The celebration, the happiness. When this was all over, when their pack was safe, and if Cade would still have him, he'd put his mark on the other wolf.

He settled in, getting comfortable against Cade's larger body. He kept his nose buried there, and Cade relaxed beneath him. Yeah, he'd make this work. He closed his eyes and willed his aching body to sleep. Cade's breathing deepened almost immediately. The steady rhythm of his chest rising and falling against Rocky's lulled him. He wiggled just a bit closer and fell asleep as well.

COMING SOON

Don't miss Soul Magic, the third book in the Triad of Magic series, coming November 12, 2019

Blood runs soul-deep, but found families are forever.

Cormac hasn't been the same since the night the High Moon Pack was attacked. With his magic weakened, he's consumed by a bloodlust he hasn't felt since he first became a vampire. His need to replenish his power makes him a danger to his last remaining family member, and his hunger makes him careless. Feeding from pack beta Liam Benson was supposed to slake his appetite, not leave him craving more.

Liam is drawn to Cormac in ways he can't explain and as the fight to protect the pack he loves reaches a critical point, his connection to Cormac deepens in a way neither wolf nor vampire anticipated. Will Cormac's role in the final showdown against the dark forces threatening the pack sever the bond Liam and Cormac have started to weave?

Simon, Gray, and Cormac must fight a being history says shouldn't exist—one with all three types of magic. The pack must use all their resources to combat the mysterious triad, even turning to the mysterious Conclave of Mages for help. As they learn more about this terrifying dark threat, protecting the pack proves to be riddled with challenges and sacrifices. While Gray attempts to hold his traumatized pack together, Cormac struggles to reconcile his past failures with his current desires, and Simon must attempt the impossible: an alliance between mind, body, and soul.

Preorder your copy today!

ABOUT THE AUTHOR

Macy Blake believes in unicorns and fairies, in moonbeams and stardust, and that happily ever after comes in all colors of the rainbow. When she's not busy at the day job, she loses herself in paranormal romance, living vicariously through her favorite sexy fictional heroes. These days you can often find her pounding away at the keyboard, trying to capture the magic of her own worlds.

Visit Macy's website
https://www.macyblake.com/

Join Macy's newsletter
http://bit.ly/MacyBlakeNews

Macy's Moonlighters Facebook Group
http://bit.ly/MacysMoonlighters

f facebook.com/macy.blake.1042

🅾 instagram.com/authormacyblake

BB bookbub.com/authors/macy-blake

ALSO BY MACY BLAKE

The Chosen One

Sweet Nothings (prequel)

All or Nothing

Nothing Ventured

Next to Nothing

Nothing Gained

Hellhound Champions

Hell On Earth

Hell To Pay

Give Him Hell

The Triad of Magic

Mind Magic

Body Magic

Soul Magic

Made in the USA
Middletown, DE
16 September 2021